J FIC WAR
Warner, Ger
From Sea to   ☐  SO-AQI-858

THE BOXCAR CHILDREN
SURPRISE ISLAND
THE YELLOW HOUSE MYSTERY
MYSTERY RANCH
MIKE'S MYSTERY
BLUE BAY MYSTERY
THE WOODSHED MYSTERY
THE LIGHTHOUSE MYSTERY
MOUNTAIN TOP MYSTERY
SCHOOLHOUSE MYSTERY
CABOOSE MYSTERY
HOUSEBOAT MYSTERY
SNOWBOUND MYSTERY
TREE HOUSE MYSTERY
BICYCLE MYSTERY
MYSTERY IN THE SAND
MYSTERY BEHIND THE WALL
BUS STATION MYSTERY
BENNY UNCOVERS A MYSTERY
THE HAUNTED CABIN MYSTERY
THE DESERTED LIBRARY MYSTERY
THE ANIMAL SHELTER MYSTERY
THE OLD MOTEL MYSTERY
THE MYSTERY OF THE HIDDEN
    PAINTING
THE AMUSEMENT PARK MYSTERY
THE MYSTERY OF THE MIXED-UP ZOO
THE CAMP-OUT MYSTERY
THE MYSTERY GIRL
THE MYSTERY CRUISE
THE DISAPPEARING FRIEND MYSTERY
THE MYSTERY OF THE SINGING GHOST
MYSTERY IN THE SNOW
THE PIZZA MYSTERY
THE MYSTERY HORSE
THE MYSTERY AT THE DOG SHOW
THE CASTLE MYSTERY
THE MYSTERY OF THE LOST VILLAGE
THE MYSTERY ON THE ICE
THE MYSTERY OF THE PURPLE POOL
THE GHOST SHIP MYSTERY

THE MYSTERY IN WASHINGTON, DC
THE CANOE TRIP MYSTERY
THE MYSTERY OF THE HIDDEN BEACH
THE MYSTERY OF THE MISSING CAT
THE MYSTERY AT SNOWFLAKE INN
THE MYSTERY ON STAGE
THE DINOSAUR MYSTERY
THE MYSTERY OF THE STOLEN MUSIC
THE MYSTERY AT THE BALL PARK
THE CHOCOLATE SUNDAE MYSTERY
THE MYSTERY OF THE HOT
    AIR BALLOON
THE MYSTERY BOOKSTORE
THE PILGRIM VILLAGE MYSTERY
THE MYSTERY OF THE STOLEN
    BOXCAR
THE MYSTERY IN THE CAVE
THE MYSTERY ON THE TRAIN
THE MYSTERY AT THE FAIR
THE MYSTERY OF THE LOST MINE
THE GUIDE DOG MYSTERY
THE HURRICANE MYSTERY
THE PET SHOP MYSTERY
THE MYSTERY OF THE SECRET MESSAGE
THE FIREHOUSE MYSTERY
THE MYSTERY IN SAN FRANCISCO
THE NIAGARA FALLS MYSTERY
THE MYSTERY AT THE ALAMO
THE OUTER SPACE MYSTERY
THE SOCCER MYSTERY
THE MYSTERY IN THE OLD ATTIC
THE GROWLING BEAR MYSTERY
THE MYSTERY OF THE LAKE MONSTER
THE MYSTERY AT PEACOCK HALL
THE WINDY CITY MYSTERY
THE BLACK PEARL MYSTERY
THE CEREAL BOX MYSTERY
THE PANTHER MYSTERY
THE MYSTERY OF THE QUEEN'S JEWELS
THE STOLEN SWORD MYSTERY
THE BASKETBALL MYSTERY

KILGORE MEMORIAL LIBRARY YORK, NE 68467

THE MOVIE STAR MYSTERY
THE MYSTERY OF THE PIRATE'S MAP
THE GHOST TOWN MYSTERY
THE MYSTERY OF THE BLACK RAVEN
THE MYSTERY IN THE MALL
THE MYSTERY IN NEW YORK
THE GYMNASTICS MYSTERY
THE POISON FROG MYSTERY
THE MYSTERY OF THE EMPTY SAFE
THE HOME RUN MYSTERY
THE GREAT BICYCLE RACE MYSTERY
THE MYSTERY OF THE WILD PONIES
THE MYSTERY IN THE COMPUTER
  GAME
THE MYSTERY AT THE CROOKED
  HOUSE
THE HOCKEY MYSTERY
THE MYSTERY OF THE MIDNIGHT DOG
THE MYSTERY OF THE SCREECH OWL
THE SUMMER CAMP MYSTERY
THE COPYCAT MYSTERY
THE HAUNTED CLOCK TOWER
  MYSTERY
THE MYSTERY OF THE TIGER'S EYE
THE DISAPPEARING STAIRCASE
  MYSTERY
THE MYSTERY ON BLIZZARD
  MOUNTAIN
THE MYSTERY OF THE SPIDER'S CLUE
THE CANDY FACTORY MYSTERY
THE MYSTERY OF THE MUMMY'S
  CURSE
THE MYSTERY OF THE STAR RUBY
THE STUFFED BEAR MYSTERY
THE MYSTERY OF ALLIGATOR SWAMP
THE MYSTERY AT SKELETON POINT
THE TATTLETALE MYSTERY
THE COMIC BOOK MYSTERY
THE GREAT SHARK MYSTERY
THE ICE CREAM MYSTERY
THE MIDNIGHT MYSTERY

THE MYSTERY IN THE FORTUNE
  COOKIE
THE BLACK WIDOW SPIDER MYSTERY
THE RADIO MYSTERY
THE MYSTERY OF THE RUNAWAY
  GHOST
THE FINDERS KEEPERS MYSTERY
THE MYSTERY OF THE HAUNTED
  BOXCAR
THE CLUE IN THE CORN MAZE
THE GHOST OF THE CHATTERING
  BONES
THE SWORD OF THE SILVER KNIGHT
THE GAME STORE MYSTERY
THE MYSTERY OF THE ORPHAN TRAIN
THE VANISHING PASSENGER
THE GIANT YO-YO MYSTERY
THE CREATURE IN OGOPOGO LAKE
THE ROCK 'N' ROLL MYSTERY
THE SECRET OF THE MASK
THE SEATTLE PUZZLE
THE GHOST IN THE FIRST ROW
THE BOX THAT WATCH FOUND
A HORSE NAMED DRAGON
THE GREAT DETECTIVE RACE
THE GHOST AT THE DRIVE-IN MOVIE
THE MYSTERY OF THE TRAVELING
  TOMATOES
THE SPY GAME
THE DOG-GONE MYSTERY
THE VAMPIRE MYSTERY
SUPERSTAR WATCH
THE SPY IN THE BLEACHERS
THE AMAZING MYSTERY SHOW
THE CLUE IN THE RECYCLING BIN
MONKEY TROUBLE

THE BOXCAR CHILDREN FROM SEA TO SHINING SEA

THE MYSTERY IN NEW YORK
THE WINDY CITY MYSTERY
THE MYSTERY IN SAN FRANCISCO

created by
GERTRUDE CHANDLER WARNER

ALBERT WHITMAN & Company
Chicago, Illinois

The Boxcar Children From Sea to Shining Sea
created by Gertrude Chandler Warner.

ISBN: 978-0-8075-0891-6

Copyright © 2011 by Albert Whitman & Company.
Published in 2011 by Albert Whitman & Company.
All rights reserved. No part of this book may be reproduced or
transmitted in any form or by any means, electronic or mechanical,
including photocopying, recording, or by any information storage and
retrieval system, without permission in writing from the publisher.
Printed in the United States of America.
THE BOXCAR CHILDREN® is a registered trademark
of Albert Whitman & Company

10 9 8 7 6 5 4 3 2 1 LB 15 14 13 12 11

Cover art by Robert Papp.

For information about Albert Whitman & Company,
visit our web site at www.albertwhitman.com.

THE MYSTERY IN NEW YORK

created by

GERTRUDE CHANDLER WARNER

Illustrated by Charles Tang

No part of this publication may be reproduced in whole or in part, or stored in a retrieval system, or transmitted in any form or by any means, electronic, mechanical, photocopying, recording, or otherwise, without written permission of the publisher. For information regarding permission, write to Albert Whitman & Company, 6340 Oakton Street, Morton Grove, IL 60053-2723.

ISBN 0-8075-5460-X

Copyright © 1999 by Albert Whitman & Company. All rights reserved. Published by Scholastic Inc., 555 Broadway, New York, NY 10012 by arrangement with Albert Whitman & Company. BOXCAR CHILDREN is a registered trademark of Albert Whitman & Company.

5 7 9 10 8 6

Printed in the U.S.A.

Contents

CHAPTER   PAGE

1. Welcome to New York   1
2. A Friendly Invitation   10
3. The Elizabeth Star   22
4. Broken Glass   38
5. A Taste for Diamonds   50
6. View from the Harbor   64
7. Trapped!   77
8. The Chase   90
9. No Joke   101
10. A Thief's Regret   112
   New York, New York! Activities   124

CHAPTER 1

Welcome to New York

"There it is! There's New York," said twelve-year-old Jessie Alden. She pressed her face to the window of the train to see the famous skyline.

"How do you know?" Henry, her fourteen-year-old brother, teased. He was sitting next to her and he leaned over to look out of the window, too.

Just then, the voice of the conductor crackled over the loudspeaker. "Next stop, New York City."

"See?" said Jessie.

Both Jessie and Henry laughed.

Behind them in the next row of seats, six-year-old Benny leaned over and whispered to the small dog in the dog carrier on the seat next to him, "We're almost there, Watch."

Watch gave a soft bark. Benny smiled and patted the carrier. Then he straightened and turned to look out the window.

Violet Alden, who was sitting between Benny and Grandfather Alden, glanced out of the window over Benny's shoulder. Then she leaned back and said to her grandfather, "New York is so *big*." Violet was ten, and she was a little timid sometimes.

Grandfather Alden patted her hand. "It's big and interesting and a lot of fun," he said. "Remember how much you liked it on your first visit?"

Violet nodded. "It *was* fun," she said.

"And we solved a mystery, too," Benny reminded her, turning back around.

"I remember. The mystery of the purple pool," Violet said. Purple was Violet's favorite color.

"You liked Mrs. Teague and her daughter, Caryn, too," Grandfather Alden went on.

"Yes. We had fun when they visited us for the Greenfield dog show," Violet agreed. She was feeling better now. "I'm glad she invited us to New York to visit her in her new apartment."

Just then the train entered a tunnel and the city disappeared from view.

"Attention, passengers," the conductor said. "Please make sure you have all your belongings before leaving the train."

A few minutes later, the train pulled into Penn Station.

The Aldens took their luggage from the baggage rack above their seats. Henry carried Watch in his dog carrier and they made their way through a maze of corridors to the information booth.

Suddenly Jessie pointed. "Look," she said. "That man is holding up a sign with our name on it."

Sure enough, a bearded man in a dark red turban and a neat driver's uniform was

holding up a sign that said ALDEN FAMILY.

"How does he know our name?" Benny asked.

"And why is he wearing that hat?" asked Violet.

"Because he's a Sikh, Violet, from northern India most likely. New York City has all kinds of people. And he knows our name because he's here to pick us up. Mrs. Teague arranged it for us. Most taxis in New York will only carry four people, so she arranged for a special car to pick us up, since there are five of us," said Grandfather.

"Six, counting Watch," Jessie said.

Grandfather shook hands with the man holding the sign and introduced himself and the Alden children.

"Pleased to meet you," the man said. "Welcome to New York. The car is this way." He led the way outdoors to a big dark blue car.

"Are we in New York City now?" asked Benny as they pulled away from the train station. All around them, cars and trucks and buses and taxis swerved and honked.

But it didn't seem to bother the driver.

"Yes, you're in the Big Apple now," he said.

Benny eagerly rolled down his window. "Hi!" he cried, waving at the people waiting at the corner.

"Oh, Benny," Jessie said. "Those people don't know you."

"It doesn't matter," Henry said. "See? They're waving back."

Sure enough, the people who were waiting at the corner for the light to change waved and smiled at Benny. Benny waved harder and held Watch up to look at the people. Watch cocked his head. Several more people waved when they saw Watch, and one woman said, "What a cute dog."

"He's smart, too," Benny called out to her as the car drove away.

"This is Central Park," the driver said. "Mrs. Teague suggested I take you on the scenic route."

"Mrs. Teague's new apartment is in a building," Grandfather added, "on the Upper West Side."

The green trees of the park rushed by. Even here, the cars and cabs honked and swerved. Everywhere the Aldens looked they saw people, all different kinds of people.

The cab turned and drove alongside the park. Then it turned again and pulled to a stop in front of a large building. A man stepped out to the curb and opened the car door for them. He wore a gray uniform with gold buttons on the jacket, gold trim on the pockets, and a matching gold-trimmed cap.

"Here we are," the driver said. He got out to help with the luggage. "Have a good visit to the city," he told the Aldens, and with a smile he touched his forehead and made a slight bow toward Benny.

"Thank you. We will," said Benny, and he touched his own forehead and bowed right back.

The driver shook hands with Grandfather. He got into his long blue car and disappeared into the rush of traffic.

Benny looked up at the man in the gray

uniform who had opened the car door. "Who are you?"

"I'm Leed," said the man, without smiling. "I'm the daytime doorman for the building. Six A.M. to two P.M."

"How do you do?" said Benny.

Mr. Leed didn't answer. In fact, he looked as if he didn't approve of Benny talking to him.

"Here. Hold on tightly to Watch's leash, Benny," Jessie said.

"I will," Benny promised. He wound Watch's leash around his fingers. Watch, who thought he was much bigger than he really was, looked eagerly around, his short tail wagging. *New York's not too big for me*, he seemed to say.

"I'm James Henry Alden," Grandfather said to Mr. Leed. "And this is Henry, Jessie, Violet, Benny, and Watch. We're here to visit Annabel Teague."

"Of course," said the doorman. He was a short, stocky man who wore gold wire-rimmed spectacles. "Mrs. Teague is expecting you."

Mr. Leed led the way into the lobby to his desk. He picked up a telephone. He dialed and then spoke into the receiver. "The Aldens are here, Mrs. Teague."

A moment later, he led them across the small lobby to the elevators. "Ninth floor, Apartment D," he said.

He touched his cap and stepped back.

"Good-bye, Mr. Leed," said Benny.

Mr. Leed didn't answer.

When the doors opened on the ninth floor, Mrs. Teague was waiting for them. In her khaki pants and navy cotton pullover sweater, with her red-gold hair pulled back into a bun, she looked almost exactly the same as the last time they had seen her. Mrs. Teague held out her hands, her blue eyes smiling. "Welcome," she said. "Welcome back to New York!"

Benny gasped as he stepped into the hall and looked past Mrs. Teague. "Uh-oh!" he cried. "What happened?"

CHAPTER 2

A Friendly Invitation

In the big room off the hall, sheets covered the furniture. Jagged holes had been punched into the walls. Some of the holes had wires hanging out. Plaster dust coated the room from floor to ceiling.

Just then a skinny man with thinning brown hair and a brown mustache came into the room. He was wearing overalls and a painter's cap that said EVANS' ELECTRIC and he was carrying a hammer. He was covered with plaster dust from his head to his shoes. He kicked up little clouds of plaster dust as he walked. Even his mustache was coated with white dust.

"I have to pick up a special tool from my shop," he said to Mrs. Teague. "I'll be back in a little while."

Jessie stared at the hammer. "Did you make all those holes in the wall?" she said to the man.

He raised one eyebrow. "Yep," he said. He lifted his hammer. "Bam, bam!" he said.

Violet jumped a little.

"Sorry," said the man. "Didn't mean to startle you." He grinned. Then he walked past the Aldens and out of the apartment.

Mrs. Teague laughed. "Arnold has an odd sense of humor, doesn't he? But yes, Jessie, he's the one who made the holes in the wall Arnold Evans is an electrician. He's been putting new electrical wiring in my apartment. He's done most of the apartment except the dining room, and he's almost finished in here."

"Oh," said Violet. She sneezed.

"I hope he finishes soon so I can put up the chandelier while you are here. It's a

beautiful old crystal one, a real antique."
Mrs. Teague raised a sheet on a side table.
Beneath it, on a blanket, lay a huge chandelier, dripping with crystal prisms of all
shapes and sizes.

"It's beautiful," said Henry.

"When I saw the smashed-in walls I
thought you had been robbed," said Benny.
"I thought it was a mystery."

Violet sneezed again.

"No mystery, Benny," said Mrs. Teague,
ruffling Benny's hair. "Not this time."

Violet sneezed a third time. Benny patted
her on the back.

Mrs. Teague said, "Let me give you a
tour." She led the Aldens through her new
apartment. It was big and filled with sunlight. A terrace outside of the living room
looked down over Central Park. "Jessie and
Violet, you'll be staying in Caryn's room.
James, you'll have the guest room, and
Benny, you and Henry will stay here in the
study. It has a foldout sofa bed."

"What about Watch?" asked Benny.

"Watch can stay wherever he likes," Mrs.

Teague said. She smiled and shook her head a little. "After all, that's what Sunny does when she's home." Sunny was the Teagues' champion show dog, a golden retriever. She was away with Mrs. Teague's daughter, Caryn, at a dog show that very week.

"Good," Benny said. "Come on, Watch. You can stay with us." Watch followed Benny and Henry into the study.

Violet went with Jessie out onto the terrace at the end of the living room. They stared down at the trees and streets spread out below them.

"Isn't Central Park lovely?" Mrs. Teague said, coming out onto the terrace where Jessie and Violet were standing.

"We drove through Central Park to get here," Jessie said. "It's even bigger than I remembered."

"It's eight hundred and forty acres," said Mrs. Teague. "Two and a half miles long and three-quarters of a mile wide. I go there often. In the winter, I like to watch the ice-skaters, and in the summer there are concerts and plays."

"Do you walk Sunny in Central Park?" Violet asked.

"Caryn or I do every day," Mrs. Teague said. "Or our dogwalker, Lydia Critt, takes Sunny out when we can't."

"A dogwalker?" Violet asked. "Is that her job?"

Mrs. Teague nodded. "She's an actress, too. But she walks dogs to make money. She has her own business, Critt's Critters. She walks other dogs in this building every day, I believe. You'll probably meet her."

"Speaking of walks," Grandfather Alden said, coming out onto the terrace to join them, "I know a little dog who'd probably like that idea."

"Come on, Violet. Let's go finish unpacking so we can take Watch out for a walk," said Jessie, smiling.

A few minutes later, the four Alden children and Watch were back in the hallway waiting for the elevator. When the doors opened on the ninth floor, a short round man with a round face and silver hair was in the elevator. His solemn face brightened when he saw the children.

He looked down at Watch as the Aldens got on. "Well, well," he said. "I don't think I've seen you in the building before."

"No," agreed Benny, who was holding Watch's leash. "We're visiting Mrs. Teague and Sunny and Caryn. But Sunny and Caryn are at a dog show. I'm Benny Alden and this is Watch."

"How do you do, Watch? How do you do, Benny?" the man said. "I'm Edgar Pound, Annabel Teague's upstairs neighbor. I'm sure you'll have fun staying with her."

Henry, Jessie, and Violet introduced themselves, too. Henry said, "Do you have a dog?"

Mr. Pound shook his head. "I'd love to have a dog, but I'm afraid I'm too busy for that. PoundStar Enterprises takes all my time. It's my company."

"Your very own company?" Violet asked.

Mr. Pound nodded. He leaned down toward Benny and opened his eyes wide. "It's named after the Elizabeth Star."

"The Elizabeth Star? What's that?" Henry wanted to know.

Mr. Pound straightened up again before he answered. "A diamond pendant. It was given to one of my late wife Kathryn's ancestors by Elizabeth I, Queen of England in the 1500s," said Mr. Pound proudly.

"So it must be pretty old," Benny said.

"Yes. It's old and beautiful. And lucky," said Mr. Pound. "It's always brought our family good fortune. . . . Well, almost always," Mr. Pound added softly as the elevator stopped. When the doors opened on the lobby, Mr. Pound motioned for the Aldens to go first. He stepped out after them.

"Good morning, Mr. Pound," said Mr. Leed, jumping up from his desk.

"Good morning, Leed," said Mr. Pound.

Mr. Leed hurried to open the heavy glass door of the building for Mr. Pound and the Aldens.

At the curb, a man in a uniform got out of a long black car and opened the door. Mr. Pound nodded at the man and got in. The car began to pull away. Then it stopped.

Mr. Pound's window hummed down. He looked out at the Aldens and motioned for them to come closer. "Would you like to see the Elizabeth Star?" he asked.

Violet's eyes widened. "Really?"

"We'd like that," Jessie said.

"Good. Then it's settled." Mr. Pound smiled. "Come see it tonight. It's in my penthouse."

"Thank you," said Henry.

Mr. Pound nodded. "I'll get in touch with Mrs. Teague to make arrangements," he said. The window of the car hummed shut and the car pulled away.

Mr. Leed, who had been standing close enough to hear the conversation, made a sour face and said, "Now, that's a bit of luck, to get a special invitation to see the Elizabeth Star. They say it's worth millions."

"Have you ever seen it?" Benny wanted to know.

"No. Why would *I* have seen it?" asked Mr. Leed. He turned abruptly and marched back inside to his desk.

"He's awfully cranky," said Jessie in a low voice to the others.

"Maybe he doesn't like his job," said Benny.

"Maybe," said Jessie. She glanced back through the heavy glass door. Mr. Leed was carefully spreading out a newspaper at his desk.

"Come on. Let's take Watch for a walk and explore a little," said Henry.

The Aldens walked to the corner and crossed the street at the crosswalk. They walked until they found an entrance in the low stone wall that bordered the park.

When they got into the park, the noise of the traffic faded. But, reaching the circular drive that went around the inside of the park, they saw plenty of traffic — people traffic! People jogging, people biking, people roller-skating and blading with headphones on, people walking, and people riding in horse-drawn carriages. Vendors sold hot dogs, pretzels, ice cream, and sodas. On benches that lined the walks, more people read newspapers and books or ate lunch. Some people just sat back with their faces tipped up to the bright afternoon sun. One man was feeding bread to a flock of pigeons.

"Woof!" Watch barked as they walked by. The flock of birds swirled quickly into the air and the man laughed and waved. The pigeons landed again almost immediately and went back to pecking at the bread the man scattered around his feet.

"Where are the cars?" asked Benny.

"According to the guidebook, cars aren't allowed in the park during the middle of the day," said Henry. "And not at all on weekends."

Benny nodded. "That's a good idea," he said. "That's what I would do if I were mayor, except I'd make all the hot dogs and ice cream and pretzels free."

"You'd get my vote, then," said Henry, and rumpled Benny's hair.

At a pond where ducks and swans swam, Watch stared intently, wagging his tail a little. But this time he didn't bark.

After they had been walking a little while,

Benny pointed. "Look, Watch," he said. "It's a statue of a dog."

Ahead was a statue of a husky, his ears up, his tail curled over his back. "It must be a famous dog," said Violet, "to have a statue."

They walked closer and read the inscription at the base.

"What does it say?" asked Benny.

"Balto," said Henry. "That's his name. It's dedicated to the sled dog team that took medicine to a village in Alaska and saved everybody in a diphtheria epidemic in 1925."

"A hero," said Violet. They looked up at the statue of the brave and noble dog.

As they walked away, Benny leaned over to pet Watch. "Keep up the good work solving mysteries," he whispered to the little dog. "Maybe one day you'll have a statue of your very own back home in Greenfield."

"Oh, Benny," said Henry. He grinned. "I don't think we're going to find any mysteries in New York City. Not on this visit."

But Henry was wrong, as they were all soon to find out.

CHAPTER 3

The Elizabeth Star

Mr. Leed was at his desk turning the pages of a dictionary when the
Aldens returned from their walk in the park
with Watch. He didn't get up to open the
door and barely looked at them before pick-
ing up his pencil and going back to his
crossword puzzle.

"Hello, Mr. Leed," said Jessie.

"Mmm," said Mr. Leed.

The elevator door opened.

"Look out!" cried Violet.

The Aldens jumped left and right as five

small black dogs with big black ears came charging out of the elevator, panting eagerly.

"Whoa! Whoaaaa!" said the young woman holding on to their leashes. The dogs slowed down a little. Then one of them saw Watch and began to bark. The other four dogs began to bark, too.

"Jim! Jack! Joe! Jill! Jinx! Be quiet!" the young woman scolded. She was a tall woman, with curly black hair, big blue eyes, and a faint scattering of freckles across her nose. She was wearing jeans, sneakers, and a gray sweatshirt that said CRITT'S CRITTERS. Crystal earrings sparkled, dangling from her ears, and another crystal hung on a silver chain around her neck.

One of the dogs touched noses with Watch. He stopped barking. Soon all the other dogs had touched noses with Watch and had stopped barking, too. All six dogs began to wag their tails and make friends.

"Cute dog," said the young woman, leaning over to pet Watch.

"Yours are cute, too," said Violet. "What kind of dogs are they?"

"Oh, they're not my dogs," said the young woman.

"I know what kind of dogs they are," said Jessie eagerly. "I remember from the Greenfield dog show: French bulldogs."

"Good guess," said the young woman.

Jessie beamed with pride.

"And I know who you are," said Henry. "Lydia Critt."

"Good guess again," the young woman said, her eyes crinkling in a smile. "But who are you? Detectives?"

"Yes, we are," said Benny.

Henry laughed and introduced everyone. "We're staying with Mrs. Teague. She said we might meet you," he told Lydia.

"And you're wearing a shirt that says " 'Critt's Critters,' " Jessie pointed out.

"That's me," Lydia said. "Dogwalker by day and actor by night. Only these days, the dog-walking business is better than the acting business." Her hand went up to her neck and she touched the crystal hanging there. "But my luck is about to change. I know it is."

"How do you know?" asked Benny.

"This crystal. It's supposed to bring good luck," she said, still touching it.

The dogs began to pull on their leashes and bark. "Oops. I've got to go. See you later," said Lydia, and she walked briskly out of the lobby.

"Lunch is soup and salad on the terrace," Mrs. Teague announced. "Mr. Evans is still working in the dining room."

The Aldens helped Mrs. Teague and Grandfather Alden set the small round table on the terrace, taking plates and silverware and food from the kitchen through the dining room.

As they did, Benny said, "Hi, Mr. Evans! You've filled up some of the holes in the wall."

"Yes," said Mr. Evans.

"I could help you make more holes in the walls," Benny offered hopefully.

"No," said Mr. Evans. "I don't think so."

He looked as if he were trying not to smile.

Behind Benny, Mrs. Teague laughed. "Why don't you give Watch some fresh water and a dog biscuit from the jar on the kitchen counter, Benny." To Mr. Evans she said, "But I will be able to use the dining room tonight, won't I? We're having a dinner guest."

Before Mrs. Teague could answer, Jessie said, "Is it Mr. Pound?"

"Right. He called and told me about his invitation to you to see his famous diamond," said Mrs. Teague. "He's going to have dinner here and then take you up to see the Elizabeth Star."

"The dining room will be finished," said Mr. Evans. "No problem."

"Great," said Mrs. Teague.

While they ate lunch, the Aldens told Grandfather and Mrs. Teague about their morning. Then Mrs. Teague told them about Mr. Pound's plans. "He wants you to come up and get him before dinner," she told the Aldens. "He's going to be working at his office at home and he *says* he sometimes loses track of time. Truth is, he loves to see children. He never had any of his own. He's been lonely since his wife died a few years ago."

"I'll go up and get him," Benny volunteered.

"I'll go with you," Jessie said.

"This evening's plans sound very exciting," Grandfather Alden said.

"Yes," agreed Benny. "Even if we don't have a mystery to solve."

"Instead of a mystery, how about a museum?" suggested Grandfather. "The American Museum of Natural History isn't far from here and it has everything from dinosaurs to whales."

"Let's go!" said Benny.

The Aldens spent the whole afternoon at the museum. Benny liked the dinosaurs. Henry liked the Hall of Ocean Life, where a life-size copy of a blue whale was suspended from the ceiling. Jessie liked the four-billion-year-old meteorite on display in the Hall of Meteorites. "It says this is the largest meteorite to ever be found on the earth's surface," she said, reading from a small plaque nearby.

Violet couldn't decide which exhibit was her favorite. "I want to see everything before I make up my mind," she declared.

"You'd have to stay here a long, long time," Grandfather told her. "The American Museum of Natural History is the largest museum of its kind in the world."

"Then I guess I like the gemstones best," Violet said. "They twinkle so, like stars of all different colors."

When the Aldens got back to the apartment building, a new doorman was on duty. This one was almost as unfriendly as Leed. He had sandy hair and bushy eyebrows. He narrowed his brown eyes and watched them as they came in.

Once again, Grandfather patiently introduced himself and the children. "And you must be the evening doorman," he said. He looked at the name tag the doorman wore. "Mr. Saunders?"

"Right," said Mr. Saunders. "Two P.M. to ten P.M. shift, weekdays."

He walked briskly back to his desk and sat down.

" 'Bye, Mr. Saunders," said Benny as they got onto the elevator.

"Good evening," said Mr. Saunders.

When they reached Mrs. Teague's apartment, they discovered that Mr. Evans had just finished plastering the last hole in the wall. The chandelier sparkled above the table. Mr. Evans folded up his ladder and propped it in a corner, while Mrs. Teague hurried around the dining room, pulling sheets off chairs.

"Thank you, Mr. Evans," said Mrs. Teague.

"I'm not finished in here," he cautioned. "I still have to paint over the patches."

"I know," she answered. "But it's finished enough for us to have dinner."

Mr. Evans shrugged. "See you tomorrow," he said, and left.

The Aldens went to work helping Mrs. Teague. They dusted tables and chairs, swept the floor, vacuumed the rug, and even wiped the mirror over the sideboard.

Then, while Violet and Henry helped Mrs. Teague set the table, Benny and Jessie went up to Mr. Pound's penthouse.

He opened the door almost as soon as they knocked. "Hello," he said.

"It's time for dinner," Benny said.

Mr. Pound looked at his watch and smiled. "It's six-thirty. You sound as if you are hungry."

"I am," said Benny.

"Too hungry to want to see the Elizabeth Star?" asked Mr. Pound.

"Right now?" Jessie said.

"Why not?" said Mr. Pound. "Come in and I'll show it to you before we go down to dinner."

So Jessie and Benny followed Mr. Pound into his penthouse — the biggest apartment in the building, on the very top floor. He led them across a large living room. One whole wall was windows, bright with the lights of the city far below.

Mr. Pound led them down a long hall

hung with paintings. He paused in front of one painting and stared at it. Jessie and Benny stopped next to him. The painting was of a beautiful woman with a kindly expression and a touch of gray in her hair. She wore a velvety blue dress that matched the color of her eyes. Mr. Pound shook his head gently as though to clear his thoughts and then walked on. Jessie and Benny exchanged glances and followed Mr. Pound down the hall.

At the end of the hall, Mr. Pound opened a door to reveal a deep closet. He pushed the coats aside and then, to the astonishment of Jessie and Benny, stepped inside!

"Come on," said Mr. Pound, and he switched on an overhead closet light.

They followed Mr. Pound and saw a keypad glowing on the wall behind the coats. It was numbered and looked like the front of a touch-tone telephone. The numbers glowed in the darkness and a small red light blinked on one side of the rows of numbers.

"What's that?" Jessie asked.

"An alarm system," Mr. Pound explained. "If anybody opens the door without punching the secret code number in, an alarm goes off here and at the alarm company. They call and if I don't answer the phone to tell them it is a false alarm, they send the police."

"A burglar alarm," said Jessie.

"What door?" asked Benny.

"You'll see," said Mr. Pound. He punched some buttons and a green light came on. "Now the alarm is off," he said. He reached up and pressed one corner of the seemingly solid wood wall.

With a quiet click, a door slid open. Mr. Pound stepped inside, turned on another light, and motioned for Benny and Jessie to follow.

The room was small, not much bigger than the closet. The walls were bare and there were no windows. In the center of the room in a glass case, a large pear-shaped diamond on a gold chain rested on a mound of blue velvet. A single overhead spotlight shone on the diamond.

"How beautiful," breathed Jessie. "It's as beautiful as any of the gems we saw in the museum today."

"It's so *big*," said Benny.

Mr. Pound nodded. "Yes," he said thoughtfully. They stared at it for a moment longer. Then Mr. Pound said, "We'd better hurry or we'll be late for dinner."

When they left, he closed the door behind them. He punched the code into the burglar alarm and the red light began to blink. Then Mr. Pound, Benny, and Jessie went down to Mrs. Teague's.

In the dining room, on the big table under the beautiful chandelier, there was a chicken dinner waiting for them. Everyone sat down. Mr. Pound was in a good mood. He laughed often and complimented Mrs. Teague on the delicious food. He asked lots of questions about the Aldens, and soon they were telling him about living in the boxcar.

"You lived in a boxcar?" Mr. Pound said. He looked amazed.

"Until Grandfather found us," Jessie said.

Taking turns, the four Alden children told Mr. Pound how, when they had first become orphans, they didn't know they had a grandfather who wanted them. So they went to live in an old abandoned boxcar in the woods. They'd had to take care of themselves.

"And then we took care of Watch, too," said Violet. "We found him, with a thorn in his paw."

"And then Grandfather found us," Henry said. "And we went to live with him in Greenfield."

"And Grandfather put the boxcar behind our house and we can visit it whenever we want," concluded Benny.

"That's some story," said Mr. Pound. He put his coffee cup in his saucer and said to Mrs. Teague, "And that was a fine meal."

"Thank you," said Mrs. Teague.

"Now, before we have dessert," said Mr. Pound, "why don't we take a break and go up to see the Elizabeth Star. Violet and Henry haven't seen it yet."

"May we bring Watch this time?" asked

Benny. "He'd like to see the diamond. Wouldn't you, Watch?"

Watch, who'd been sitting politely on his dog pillow just inside the entrance to the kitchen, stood up and barked once as if to say, *Yes*.

"Of course Watch can come," said Mr. Pound.

"Wait till you see it," Benny said in a hushed voice as they stepped off the elevator. He and Jessie had naturally told the others about getting to see the diamond before dinner.

As they crossed the penthouse living room, a clock began to chime. "Eight o'clock," said Mr. Pound. He led the way to the closet. He glanced at the painting of the lady in blue, but he didn't stop. Once again, he punched numbers into the burglar alarm as Benny and Jessie explained how the alarm worked.

"A secret door," Henry said in surprise.

"It's warm in here," said Mr. Pound, wiping his forehead. "Now, the Elizabeth Star is priceless," he continued as he slid the door to the windowless room open. "You can't be too careful when . . ."

He stepped into the tiny room, but he never finished the sentence. The alarm began to clang so loudly that Violet clapped her hands over her ears.

Watch barked and tugged so hard on his leash, he almost pulled Benny over.

Mr. Pound turned, his handkerchief raised to his pale forehead. "It's gone!" he shouted. "The Elizabeth Star has been stolen!"

CHAPTER 4

Broken Glass

At that moment, the phone began to ring. Mr. Pound spun around and pushed his way out of the closet. He stumbled over Watch's leash somehow. Watch broke loose.

"Watch!" cried Benny.

Mr. Pound raced to the phone and snatched up the receiver. "Call the police," he shouted into the phone. "I've been robbed."

"That must be the alarm company calling," said Jessie.

Benny ran after Watch. Grandfather and Mrs. Teague tried to help him catch the excited barking dog. Violet kept her hands over her ears and backed away from the awful shrieking noise of the alarm.

Someone began pounding on the front door.

"Get the door!" Mr. Pound called.

Jessie and Henry raced to the front door and Jessie threw it open. Mr. Saunders stood there.

"What happened? What's wrong?" he demanded. "The alarm went off!"

"Mr. Pound has been robbed," Henry said.

Now Mr. Saunders's bushy red eyebrows shot upward. Then he said, "Robbed? Not the . . . not the Elizabeth Star?"

"Yes," said Jessie, loudly enough to be heard over all the noise.

"But—that's impossible. No one has been in or out of this building all evening except the people who live here and their guests," said Mr. Saunders.

Just then, the alarm stopped. Jessie and

Henry turned and saw Mr. Pound emerge from the closet. He took out his handkerchief and wiped his face again, then wadded it back into his jacket pocket. "The police are on their way," he said. "I just turned off the alarm."

Mr. Saunders crossed the room. "It was in the closet?" he asked.

"In a hidden room behind a secret door at the back of the closet," said Violet, who had just stopped holding her hands over her ears.

Mr. Saunders went closer to the closet and leaned to peer inside, where Benny was kneeling by Watch, patting his head. "There *is* a hidden room!" he exclaimed.

"We'd better not touch anything," Mr. Pound told them. "The police will want to check for clues."

"Right," said Mr. Saunders, straightening up. "Well, I'd better get back downstairs."

Mr. Saunders hurried out. A moment later, two police officers pushed through the open door. More police officers followed, and soon it seemed as if there were police officers everywhere, taking photographs and asking questions.

As the officers talked to Mr. Pound, Jessie went to the secret door and looked inside. The glass case stood on a small table. A switch by the door turned on the light that shone directly on the empty blue velvet inside the case where the diamond had been. The top of the glass case was shattered and glass sparkled on the velvet and on the plain wood floor.

Henry and Violet came up to stand next to Jessie. "No windows," Henry noted.

"No," Violet agreed. "No way in or out except through this door."

"Step aside, please," a pleasant, calm voice said. They turned to see a police officer with a camera. "I have to take photographs of the crime scene," she went on.

The Aldens moved away.

Out in the living room, Mr. Pound was sitting on the sofa, talking to two other police officers. "No," he said as Jessie, Henry, and Violet approached. "No, I punched in the code and pushed open the door and the

alarm went off. That's when I saw the glass case had been broken."

"Maybe the alarm isn't working right," suggested Jessie.

The two police officers and Mr. Pound looked over at her. Mr. Pound's eyes darted back and forth and he clutched his handkerchief in his fist.

"Maybe," said one of the officers. "That's one explanation." She looked at Mr. Pound. "And the last time you saw the diamond was when you opened the safe room earlier this evening?"

"Yes, Officer." Mr. Pound nodded and motioned toward Jessie. "She was with me and saw the Elizabeth Star. So did her little brother."

"Is this true?" the policewoman asked Jessie.

"Yes," said Jessie. "It is . . . it was . . . a beautiful diamond."

The policewoman made a note in her notebook and nodded at her fellow officer. He closed his notebook, too. "We don't have any more questions right now," he said. "But we need to dust for fingerprints and take more measurements and photographs and do a thorough search of the apartment and the common areas of the building."

"Search?" Mr. Pound's voice quavered.

"For evidence, clues. You never know what will turn up," said the policeman.

Mrs. Teague, who had been standing to one side with Grandfather Alden, said, "Edgar, why don't you come back to my apartment for a nice cup of hot tea."

"And dessert," Benny said suddenly. "We still haven't had dessert."

"Oh, Benny," said Violet, putting her hand on her little brother's shoulder.

"It might make you feel better," Benny went on. "It's chocolate cake with chocolate frosting."

Mr. Pound mopped his forehead and managed a wan smile. "Maybe it will," he said to Benny. To Mrs. Teague he said, "Thank you. Maybe it would be best if I got away from all this."

"Sounds like a good idea," said the policewoman. "We have Mrs. Teague's apartment and phone numbers so we can reach you if we need you."

The Aldens, Mrs. Teague, and Mr. Pound returned to the apartment. Mr. Pound sank down heavily onto the sofa.

"Just sit down and relax," said Mrs. Teague.

Grandfather Alden and Violet sat down with him to keep him company, while Jessie, Benny, and Henry went with Mrs. Teague to help make tea.

"I don't feel at all well," said Mr. Pound. "This is terrible, just terrible." He mopped his face and tugged at the collar of his shirt. "Maybe a glass of ice water . . ." His voice trailed off.

Violet stood up. "I'll get it for you," she said.

"Yes, thank you, Violet. That might help," Mr. Pound said gratefully. He shivered and looked around.

"The door to the terrace is open," said Grandfather Alden. "I'll close it." He got up and hurried out.

A moment later, Mrs. Teague returned with the tea tray. She found Mr. Pound standing in the dining room by the dinner table. He looked almost like he'd been walking in his sleep.

"Is there anything wrong, Edgar?"

"What?" he said, surprised to see her. "No . . . no, nothing's wrong. Let me help you with the tea tray," he added quickly.

They returned to the living room.

"Here's your water," said Violet.

"Thank you," said Mr. Pound. "I feel better now." He shook his head. "I just don't understand how it happened. Why didn't the alarm work before, when the thief took the diamond?"

"Maybe the thief didn't use the door. Maybe there's another secret door into the room," said Benny. "Maybe someone sneaked in through that and took the diamond."

"No. There are no secret doors or windows," said Mr. Pound. "I had that room built especially for the Elizabeth Star. The only way in or out was through that door in the back of the closet."

"Have you had the alarm long?" asked Henry.

"Two years," said Mr. Pound. "I have it checked once a year. I just had it checked a few weeks ago. It was working fine."

"Maybe someone sneaked into the room and hid, and then took the diamond," suggested Benny.

But Jessie said, "No. There was nowhere to hide in that room. It was too small."

"And how would anyone get out without setting off the alarm?" added Violet.

"They could if the alarm wasn't working right," said Henry. "And it wasn't. It started ringing *after* Mr. Pound punched in the code."

"That's true," said Mr. Pound. "Someone must have tampered with it." He paused, then said, "The police will know."

"We'll find out," Benny said. "Don't worry. We're very good at solving mysteries. We'll solve this one for you."

Benny had said this before about other mysteries, and he had been right before. But Mr. Pound didn't know that. He smiled at Benny. "That's very kind of you, young man. But leave solving mysteries to the police."

He wiped his face one last time, then smoothed his handkerchief out and folded it up and tucked it into his pocket. He stood up. "Thank you again for all your help. And for the delicious dinner."

"Of course," said Mrs. Teague.

She and Grandfather Alden walked with Mr. Pound to the front door. The children gathered up the plates and saucers and teacups and took them into the kitchen to wash them.

"I don't think Mr. Pound believed me when I told him we could solve the mystery," Benny said. He put a teacup carefully on the counter.

"I don't think he did, either, Benny," agreed Jessie.

"It's going to be a hard mystery to solve," said Violet. "The Elizabeth Star was in a room without windows and only one door. No one went in or out until we got there. And no one went in or out of the building except residents and their guests, according to the doorman."

"But someone did go into that locked room without setting off the alarm. And whoever it was took the diamond. We'll have a lot of work to do, to figure this mystery out," Henry said.

"We will," said Jessie confidently. "We'll start first thing tomorrow morning."

CHAPTER 5

A Taste for Diamonds

"Mr. Leed," said Jessie the next morning when the Aldens came downstairs after breakfast. "May we ask you some questions?"

"Do you need directions to somewhere in the city?" asked Mr. Leed. He had a fresh newspaper spread out in front of him and was doing the crossword puzzle.

"No. We're working on the mystery," said Benny.

"Mystery?" said Mr. Leed. "What mystery?"

"That one," said Henry, pointing at the headline of the newspaper. It said, TWIN-KLE, TWINKLE, ELIZABETH STAR, WE ALL WONDER WHERE YOU ARE.

"Oh," said Mr. Leed. "Interesting."

"Yes. It is. We were in Mr. Pound's penthouse when the diamond was stolen," said Benny.

"You were?" Mr. Leed looked startled.

"Not exactly," Jessie said quickly. "We were there when Mr. Pound discovered it had been stolen. And we want to help him get it back. So we were wondering if we could look at your logbook. You know, the book where everyone who doesn't live here and isn't a guest has to sign in and out."

For a long moment, Mr. Leed looked at them. Then he pushed the logbook toward them, flipped the pages back, and said, "Here's the log from yesterday."

"We want to look at who signed in and signed out last night," Jessie said. "Between six-thirty and eight o'clock. That's when the robbery happened."

"Go ahead," said Mr. Leed. "I don't know what you expect to find."

"You never know," said Jessie. They bent over the logbook.

Running her finger down the page, Violet said, "Someone delivered pizza to Apartment 6E at six-thirty and signed out at six-forty-five."

Henry took a notebook out of his pocket and wrote it down. Jessie said, "And Lydia was here at six-forty-five. She took the dogs out for Apartment 3W at six-fifty. She came back at seven-twenty, but didn't sign out again until seven-fifty."

"That's a long time," said Violet as Henry wrote this down, too. "Thirty minutes. Hmmm."

"And then no one else," said Jessie.

"Sounds like a quiet night. Saunders was lucky," said Mr. Leed.

The Aldens looked amazed. "A quiet night!" cried Benny. "But the diamond got stolen."

"Oh," said Mr. Leed. "Right."

Henry had one more question. "If you

leave the desk, can anyone come in the door?"

"Of course not!" Now Mr. Leed looked indignant. "We lock the door if we have to leave the front desk. And we're never gone more than five minutes."

"Thank you," said Jessie. She turned and led the way back to the elevator.

"Where are we going?" Violet whispered as the elevator doors closed behind them.

"Benny and I are going to 6E to see if pizza really was delivered there last night. Because if it wasn't, maybe it was just a trick to get into the building to steal the diamond."

"Right," said Henry. "And Violet and I can go to 3W and see if Lydia walked the dogs last night — and why it took her so long to leave. She could have taken the diamond then."

"We'll meet out front in twenty minutes," said Jessie as the elevator doors opened on the third floor.

"Okay," said Henry.

Henry and Violet walked to 3W and

knocked on the door. A moment later, they heard small bodies thumping against the door and the muffled sound of barking. But no one answered.

Henry knocked again, harder. The barking grew louder. But still no one answered.

"I guess whoever lives there has gone to work," said Henry. "We'll have to come back later to ask about Lydia."

Meanwhile, Jessie and Benny had found someone home in Apartment 6E. A sleepy-looking man with shaving cream on half his face opened the door. He yawned when he saw them and said, "What is this? Halloween trick or treat?"

"No," said Jessie. "We're visiting Mrs. Teague on the ninth floor."

"Congratulations," said the man. He yawned again and started to close the door.

"Wait," said Benny. "We want to ask you a question."

"Ah," said the man. "Trick or *question*. Okay, ask your question."

"Did you order pizza last night?"

"I did. Everything, hold-the-anchovies.

My usual from the corner pizza. Why?" Now he didn't look quite so sleepy.

Jessie explained about the missing diamond. "We're trying to help Mr. Pound find out who took it," she said. "And we wanted to make sure that someone really delivered pizza to your apartment."

"He sure did. Leo. He's been delivering pizza to me for a few years now. Paying his way through college. He had to wait while I found money to pay for it. That's why it took him so long," the man said.

"Thank you," Jessie said.

"You're welcome," the man said, and closed the door.

Downstairs, Jessie and Benny found Henry and Violet sitting on the low wall around one of the flower beds outside the building.

"The pizza man didn't do it," said Benny. "He's a real pizza man, not a diamond thief."

"No one was home where the French bulldogs live," reported Henry. "So we couldn't find out if Lyd—"

"Shhh," said Jessie. She waved. "Hi, Lydia," she said.

They all looked up and saw Lydia striding down the sidewalk.

"Good morning," said Lydia. "Can't stop to talk. The dogs are waiting." She hurried by.

When she passed, Henry said, "I know what we should do. Let's follow Lydia after she walks the dogs. Maybe she will act suspicious."

"Let's go across the street to the park," suggested Violet. "We can watch for Lydia there and she won't see us."

So that is what they did. They waited until Lydia had returned from walking the five French bulldogs. Then they followed her as she left Mrs. Teague's building.

The Aldens trailed after Lydia as she strolled along the park. At the bottom of the park she turned left. She walked across to Fifth Avenue and turned right, heading downtown. A few blocks later she stopped to stare into a window.

"Tiffany's," said Jessie. "It's a very famous jewelry store."

Sure enough, even from where they stood, hiding behind a mailbox and lamppost, the Aldens could see lots and lots of diamonds and pearls and all kinds of precious jewels on display in the windows of the store.

"Maybe she is going to try to sell the diamond to them," said Violet.

But Henry shook his head. "No. A famous store like Tiffany's would never buy a stolen diamond. Lydia would have to sell it secretly to someone dishonest."

"Maybe she wants to buy fancy jewelry when she sells the diamond and she is just window-shopping now," Jessie said. "Something even nicer than her crystal necklace."

"Or maybe she's just trying to figure out how much the Elizabeth Star is worth," added Violet.

Lydia leaned over to look more closely at something in the window. Then she straightened up and walked into Tiffany's.

The Aldens exchanged glances.

"Come on," said Henry.

They walked into Tiffany's after Lydia, and stopped.

The whole place seemed to glitter. What seemed like endless rows of glass cases filled the room, each glimmering with diamonds, emeralds, and rubies, along with silver and gold.

"Wow," said Benny, his eyes round.

"Look," Violet said softly. "That lady has her dog with her."

A tall, elegant woman was tucking a robin's-egg-blue box into a Tiffany's shopping bag. Over one shoulder was a large square leather purse and sure enough, sitting in the purse, peering back at the Aldens, was a small, silky-haired brown dog with bright button eyes and a bow on its head.

"We could have brought Watch to Tiffany's," Benny said.

"Shhh! There's Lydia," whispered Jessie.

Just ahead of them, Lydia had stopped in front of a counter and was leaning down.

"Those are diamonds in that case," Violet breathed.

But Lydia didn't stay long by the sparkling display. She stepped back and continued to wander up and down the aisles.

"She's looking at the people in here as much as she's looking at the jewels," said Henry thoughtfully. "It's almost as if she is studying them."

Violet's eyes widened. "Maybe she's planning another robbery. Maybe she's going to see what someone buys, then follow that person home and steal it!"

A moment later, Lydia walked around a display case that glittered with gold. As the Aldens started to follow her, a large man in a dark suit stepped into their path. "Look at this, dear," he said to a woman with a bored expression who stood nearby. He didn't even seem to notice the Aldens.

Quickly, they ducked around the large man, just in time to see Lydia vanishing through a side door that led onto the street.

"She's getting away," gasped Jessie. They

rushed to the door and out—and stopped.

Lydia was gone. She had vanished into the crowds that streamed past them on the sidewalk.

"Do you think she knew we were following her?" asked Benny a little while later.

Henry shook his head. He couldn't answer because he had a mouthful of hot dog and mustard.

"Me either," Benny agreed, taking a bite of his own hot dog. "She never even looked back once. Have you ever noticed how people never look back? That's why they're so easy to follow."

The Aldens were eating lunch. They had bought hot dogs from a park vendor and found a spot on a bench above Wollman Rink in Central Park. As they ate, they watched the people roller-skating and blading in the rink below and talked about the mystery.

"Lydia is our best suspect," said Jessie. "And she *was* acting a little oddly in Tiffany's."

"But that doesn't make her a thief," Violet said.

Henry said, "If she's not the thief, then someone else is. But there were no strangers in the building last night, according to Mr. Saunders. And no one else signed in or out."

They munched on in thoughtful silence. Benny had finished his hot dog and was watching Violet finish hers when Jessie broke the spell.

"What if Mr. Saunders isn't telling the truth? What if he let someone in?"

"Maybe he did," said Henry.

"Or maybe he did it himself," said Benny.

"I don't think so, Benny. He can't leave his desk for very long, because he locks the front door when he does. If he did that, someone would have noticed."

"That's true," agreed Violet. "I don't think Mr. Saunders could have been away from his desk long enough to break into Mr. Pound's apartment, get into the secret room, and steal the diamond."

"What about Mr. Pound? Maybe he did

it. Maybe he took the diamond earlier in the evening and then just pretended that it was stolen when we got there," said Jessie. She paused, then shook her head. "No, that couldn't have happened. We saw it when we went upstairs to get Mr. Pound for dinner."

"Right," said Benny.

Henry finished his hot dog and stood up. "We don't have many clues. I think we need to ask more questions. And I think we need to start with Mr. Pound."

CHAPTER 6

View from the Harbor

Henry called Mrs. Teague from a pay phone on a corner and told her that they were going to Mr. Pound's office to ask some more questions about the mystery of the missing diamond. Then he called information and got Mr. Pound's office address. Finally, he looked in his guidebook and discovered that a nearby bus would take them to Wall Street, near Mr. Pound's office.

"Wall Street is named after a real wall that used to be where the street is today," he told the others as they sat down on the wide seat at the back of the bus. Fortunately, it wasn't very crowded. "It was made by the Dutch settlers out of big wood planks."

"Why?" asked Violet.

"To protect the early settlers from attack," Henry said. "That was in 1653 and New York wasn't a big city like it is today. It was just a settlement with a few dozen people."

"And now it has so many," said Jessie in amazement.

"In a very small area," Henry said. "My guidebook says that the island of Manhattan is only 13.4 miles long and 2.3 miles wide at the widest point."

The bus was driving down a street that was narrow, with buildings so tall they seemed to lean over it. It was almost as if the bus had driven into a tunnel.

"This is Wall Street, our stop," said Henry.

They got off the bus. The men and women hurrying by seemed to all be wearing dark suits and worried expressions.

Most of them carried briefcases. When the children reached Mr. Pound's office, a guard made them sign in at a desk in the lobby. Then they rode an elevator up to the twenty-third floor. They stepped off the elevator and saw a pair of glass doors with silver handles in front of them. POUNDSTAR was written in golden script across the door.

Jessie led the way, pushing open the doors and stopping in front of the receptionist's desk. "We're here to see Mr. Pound," she announced.

"Do you have an appointment?" asked the receptionist.

"No," said Jessie.

"We're here to help him find his diamond," Benny said.

The receptionist raised an eyebrow. "Really?" she said. "And which detective agency shall I tell Mr. Pound's secretary you are from?"

"The Alden Family Detective Agency," said Henry firmly. "We'll be glad to wait."

He went and sat down on one of the plush wine-colored chairs in the reception area. He folded his arms. Jessie, Benny, and Violet did the same.

The receptionist picked up the phone. "Some children who say they are from the Alden Family Detective Agency are here to see Mr. Pound. They say it is about the stolen diamond."

A moment later, the receptionist's expression of polite scorn changed to one of surprise. She put down the phone. "Mr. Pound will see you now," she said. She pointed. "Go down the hall, then up the stairs. He'll meet you at the top."

"Thank you," said Violet.

The receptionist just stared at them.

"What's this? You've found my diamond?" Mr. Pound called from the top of the stairs where he was waiting. He smiled, but his eyes looked worried.

"No," said Jessie. "Not yet."

"Ahh," said Mr. Pound. "Well, why don't you step into my office."

In the office, which had windows that went from the floor to the ceiling, the Aldens sat down in chairs facing Mr. Pound across his large desk. On the wall behind him hung a familiar-looking portrait.

"That looks like the same lady as in the painting in your apartment — and she's wearing the Elizabeth Star," said Benny.

"Yes," said Mr. Pound quietly. "That's my late wife, Kathryn. She wore the Star as often as she could. She always said it was one of nature's lovely things and shouldn't be shut up. She thought everyone should have a chance to see it."

"But *no* one will have a chance to see it again if we don't solve this mystery," said Violet softly.

Mr. Pound looked at Violet. Her words had made him suddenly quiet and thoughtful, and the children waited a moment before speaking again.

"We wanted to ask you a few more questions," Henry said, breaking the silence.

"Ah," said Mr. Pound. "Certainly. Go ahead."

"Does anyone else know the security code?" asked Jessie.

"No," said Mr. Pound. "Only me."

"Do you know if anyone tampered with the alarm?" asked Henry.

Mr. Pound paused. Then he shook his head. "It's very strange," he said. "But the police don't believe that there is anything wrong with the alarm. The security company doesn't think so, either, although they are not so sure. A real expert might have been able to fix it so it didn't go off while he took the diamond . . . but they don't think it is possible. I don't understand it."

"Has anyone else been working on anything in your apartment?" asked Jessie. "Anyone who could have tampered with the alarm or found out the code somehow?"

Again Mr. Pound shook his head. "No. My housekeeper comes in every day, of course, but she's worked for me for twenty years. She's very honest. The police have already cleared her. She was with her son and his wife and her new granddaughter all night."

"Did the police find any suspicious fingerprints?" asked Benny.

"No, Benny," said Mr. Pound. "I'm afraid not."

"Has Lydia Critt ever been to your apartment?" asked Jessie.

Now Mr. Pound looked surprised. "The dogwalker? No. She'd have no reason to. I don't have a dog."

The Aldens exchanged glances. Then Jessie said, "Mr. Pound. Could we go look at the scene of the crime again?"

"The scene of the crime? You mean the secret room where I kept the Elizabeth Star?"

"Yes," said Jessie.

"Well . . ." said Mr. Pound. At last he said, "I don't see why not. The alarm's not on. No reason for it to be." He looked at his watch. "My housekeeper is leaving in a little while, but I'll call her and tell her to leave a spare key with Mr. Saunders for you."

"Thanks," said Jessie.

Standing up, Henry said, "Thank you for seeing us, Mr. Pound."

"And don't worry," Benny added. "We'll find the Elizabeth Star."

Mr. Pound shook his head. But he looked

less worried as he walked with them back to the stairs. "Well," he said, "good luck."

Since they were downtown, the Aldens walked over to the Staten Island ferry and rode it over to Staten Island and back, past the Statue of Liberty. Benny waved at the statue as the ferry went by. They admired the famous skyline of the city, with its sky-scrapers and distinctive buildings sharp against the glowing sky.

"New York looks different," said Benny.

"Different from what, Benny?" asked Violet.

"Different from the way it looked when we went to the top of the Empire State Building the last time we were here," said Benny.

"Everything seems to change all the time in New York," said Violet. "It's very confusing."

"Not as confusing as this mystery," said Jessie a little crossly. "It looks different from every angle."

Henry patted her shoulder. "It was a good idea to ask to visit Mr. Pound's

apartment again. Maybe we'll find a clue there."

Jessie looked a little more cheerful. "Maybe," she said. "I hope so."

"Thank you, Mr. Saunders," said Benny as the doorman slid the key across the lobby desk.

"You're welcome. Bring it back when you are finished," said Mr. Saunders, "so I can give it to Mr. Pound. Those were my instructions."

"We will," Violet promised. "We just want to look for clues."

"To solve the theft of the diamond?" asked Mr. Saunders.

"Yes," said Henry.

"Well," said Mr. Saunders. He paused. "It certainly makes this building look bad, a theft like that happening here." He made a face. "It's in all the newspapers. Reporters have been snooping around all day."

"Did you talk to any of them?" asked Benny.

"No! Certainly not," said Mr. Saunders.

He looked past Benny. "Sign out, please," he said.

Mr. Evans, who had come up behind the Aldens, said, "I know, I know," and bent to sign the log.

"Hi, Mr. Evans," said Benny. "Are you finished work for today?"

"For today, yes," said Mr. Evans. "But an electrician is never short on work." He looked at Benny. "That's a joke."

"Oh," said Benny.

"Very amusing," said Mr. Saunders without smiling.

Mr. Evans rolled his eyes.

"Come on, Benny," said Violet. "Let's go to Mr. Pound's apartment."

The apartment was dark and quiet. "It's scary in here," said Benny. "What if the thief is hiding somewhere, waiting for us?"

"Don't worry, Benny," Jessie told her younger brother. "The thief doesn't know we are here. How could he?"

"He could if he was Mr. Saunders," said Benny stubbornly.

"Even if he is Mr. Saunders, he can't do anything to us," said Jessie. But she looked around nervously and all four of the Alden children moved closer together.

Henry turned on the light in the hall, and then he turned on the light in the closet. Just as Mr. Pound had said, the alarm wasn't on. He pushed open the secret door and Jessie turned on the single spotlight that illuminated the room. The glass from the broken case covered the floor.

Henry went over and carefully lifted the shattered glass lid.

"Be careful not to cut yourself," Jessie warned.

"I will," he said, frowning. "Why—" he began.

But he didn't get to finish his sentence.

The door of the secret room slammed heavily shut behind the Aldens.

"Hey!" said Benny. He ran to the door and hit it with his fists. It didn't budge.

"There's no doorknob," said Violet.

"It must have a hidden catch, just like on the other side," said Henry.

But before they could look for the hidden catch that would unlock the door, the light went out.

They were locked in the secret room in total darkness.

CHAPTER 7

Trapped!

"Oh, no!" cried Violet.

"Help!" shouted Benny. "Help! Help!" He hit the door with his fists.

"That won't work, Benny," said Jessie as she walked forward and bumped into something soft.

"Ow!" said Violet.

"It's me," Jessie said. "Sorry, Violet."

Violet held on to Jessie's arm. "Benny," said Jessie.

"I'm here," said Benny, and bumped hard into his two sisters.

"Oof," said Jessie.

"I'm *not* scared," said Benny, grabbing Jessie's other arm.

"Good," said Henry's voice in the darkness behind them. "I'm not, either. We don't need light to try to find the secret catch on the door. Remember? Mr. Pound had to find it by using his fingers to feel it."

"That's right," said Jessie.

"I think this is the door," said Henry. "I'm going to start over here." From the sound of his voice, Jessie could tell that Henry had moved away from her.

"I'll start over here," she said. She moved along the wall where she thought the door was in the opposite direction. It wasn't easy, with both Violet and Benny holding on to her so tightly.

Jessie ran her fingers over the cool, smooth wood. It all felt the same. Then she felt something. "I found the light switch," she said. But when she clicked it, nothing happened. The darkness was as thick as ever.

Violet said, "Mr. Pound knows we're here. He'll come and get us if we can't get out."

"Mr. Saunders knows, too," Jessie reminded her.

She felt Violet's grip loosen. Then Violet said, "Benny, come help me look for the hidden catch."

Benny let go of Jessie. "Okay," he said. "I've got both hands on the wall."

"Then run your fingers along the wall and press down and see if it makes the door open," said Violet. "Sort of like a magic door."

"Like a magic door," echoed Benny.

"Remember there's broken glass in the room," said Henry. "Stay close to the wall."

The Aldens worked in silence. For a long, long time, it seemed, nothing happened.

Then Violet drew in a sharp breath. "I think I've got it," she said.

They heard a click — and then the door swung open.

"It's dark out here," Violet said.

"The light in the hall isn't working, either," said Henry, flicking the switch.

Suddenly Jessie let out a little shriek as a

shape loomed out of the shadows.

"Don't shout like that," said a familiar voice. "You scared me."

"Mr. Saunders!" Jessie gasped. "What are you doing here?"

Mr. Saunders looked cranky. "I came to see what was keeping you so long."

"Someone locked us in the closet and turned out the lights," said Jessie. "That's what took us so long."

Peering at Jessie suspiciously through his glasses, Mr. Saunders said, "In the closet? What are you talking about? The closet door was open when I came in."

"Not in the closet. In the secret room at the back of the closet," said Henry, and explained what happened. When Henry had finished, Mr. Saunders shook his head.

"I don't know *how* you managed to lock yourselves up in there," he said.

"We didn't!" Benny said indignantly.

Mr. Saunders ignored him. "And I don't know why you turned off the main fuse in the apartment."

"We didn't," Benny said again, even more

outraged. He paused, then said, "What's a main fuse?"

With a sigh, Mr. Saunders said, "Come on." He led the way through the shadowy apartment into the kitchen. In the kitchen pantry he opened the door of a small metal box and pointed to what looked like a row of switches. "Every apartment has a fuse box. That's the box that controls the electricity that comes into the apartment. If you turn off this main switch at the bottom of the fuse box, it turns off all the electricity coming into an apartment," he explained.

Mr. Saunders reached out and flicked the main switch.

Lights came on in Mr. Pound's apartment.

The doorman looked down and frowned. "And it looks like someone spilled flour in here," he said, shaking his head in disapproval.

"We didn't," Benny said for a third time.

Violet sneezed.

"Mr. Saunders," said Henry, "how did you know where the fuse box was?"

"I've been the doorman here for twelve

years. There's not a lot I don't know about this building, like the fact that the fuse boxes are in the same place in every apartment," Mr. Saunders answered. "Now come on. Let's go. I have to get back to my desk. It's almost five o'clock, one of the busiest times of my day."

Violet sneezed and Henry patted her on the back.

No one said anything as they followed Mr. Saunders out of the apartment.

The elevator stopped. The doors opened.

Lydia Critt got on. "Hello," she said cheerfully.

"Hi," Jessie said. "Where are the French bulldogs?"

"Oh, I don't walk them until tonight," said Lydia. "I'm just here to meet a new dog-walking client." She touched the crystal that glinted at her neck. "See? This crystal *does* bring good luck."

The doors opened again at Mrs. Teague's floor. "See you later," Lydia said.

"Yes," said Henry.

"Wait a minute," said Mr. Saunders. He

held out his hand. "The key to Mr. Pound's apartment, please."

Henry gave him back the key.

When the elevator door had closed, Violet said, "I don't think he believed anything we said."

"Or maybe he was only pretending he didn't," said Henry.

"Well, if he's just pretending to be cranky, too, he's doing a very good job," said Jessie.

"Maybe Mr. Saunders is the one who locked us in the secret room. Maybe he followed us upstairs and closed the door and turned off the lights," Henry answered.

Violet said slowly, "If he did it, he must have been trying to scare us."

"Not me," Benny crowed. "He didn't scare me."

"That's right," said Jessie. "And the only reason he would want to scare us is to try to keep us from solving the mystery."

"Does that mean Mr. Saunders is the thief?" asked Benny.

"He's the only one besides Mr. Pound

who knew where we were," said Violet.

"Unless Lydia knew, somehow," said Jessie. "Maybe, if she and Mr. Saunders are working together, he told her and she went up and locked us in the secret room and turned off the lights."

"That's right!" said Violet. "Lydia could have done it. And then Mr. Saunders could have come up to save us, so we wouldn't suspect him."

"Or it could have been someone else who also knew where we were," said Henry. He stopped in front of the door to Mrs. Teague's apartment and fumbled in his pocket for the key. "Someone who would know where to find an electric fuse box."

"Who?" asked Benny.

"Think, Benny," said Henry. "Who else was standing at the front desk, signing out, when we got the key for Mr. Pound's apartment?"

Benny's eyes grew round. "Mr. Evans!" he cried.

At that moment, the door of Mrs. Teague's apartment swung open.

"Mr. Evans!" gasped Violet.

Had he heard them? He didn't seem to have. He smiled. "Hello again," he said. To Mrs. Teague, who was holding the door for him, he said, "Silly of me to have forgotten my tools like that. Well, see you tomorrow."

"You *will* be finished tomorrow, won't you?" asked Mrs. Teague.

"Oh, yes," said Mr. Evans. "Don't worry."

He nodded pleasantly at the Aldens and walked down the hall toward the elevator.

"What's Mr. Evans doing here?" asked Henry.

"He came back. He forgot some of his tools," said Mrs. Teague.

The Aldens exchanged glances. Was that the reason Mr. Evans had come back? Or was it only an excuse so that he could sneak upstairs and lock them in the secret room?

Shortly after dinner, they heard a knock at the door.

Mrs. Teague opened it and said in a surprised voice, "Edgar Pound. Come in."

"I hope I'm not interrupting anything," said Mr. Pound. "I came to see if our young detectives had any luck finding new clues in the apartment this afternoon."

He smiled at the Aldens.

"No luck yet," said Jessie.

"Oh," said Mr. Pound. "Too bad." But he didn't sound very sorry.

"Have the police had any luck?" asked Henry.

"No. Not yet," said Mr. Pound. "I'm beginning to think the Elizabeth Star is gone forever." He took out his handkerchief and mopped his forehead.

"Sit down and join us for a cup of tea," said Mrs. Teague.

"Thank you. I think I will," said Mr. Pound. He started toward the dining room.

"Why don't we sit in the living room," suggested Mrs. Teague. "It'll be more comfortable."

After they had finished their tea, Mr. Pound stood up. Holding his teacup in his hand, he began to walk through the dining room to the kitchen.

"I'll take your cup for you, Mr. Pound," offered Henry.

"Oh, no. No, I'm fine," said Mr. Pound, holding on to the cup.

"But — "

Mr. Pound ignored Henry. He marched into the kitchen and put the cup down. Henry went back to help gather up the rest of the cups and saucers.

He reached the dining room to find Mr. Pound holding one of the dining room chairs, which he pulled out from the table.

"Mr. Pound?" said Henry.

"Oh!" Mr. Pound jumped. "I just thought I'd sit down for a moment." He sat down.

"Are you all right, Edgar?" asked Mrs. Teague, bustling into the dining room.

"I'm fine. Don't worry about me. Just go on and do what you were doing," insisted Mr. Pound.

The Aldens cleared away the dishes, walking back and forth as Mr. Pound sat in the dining room chair.

When Benny had finished helping, he sat down in a dining room chair across from Mr. Pound.

"What are you doing, Benny?" asked Violet.

"Keeping Mr. Pound company so he doesn't get lonely," said Benny.

"You don't need to do that, Benny," said Mr. Pound.

"It's okay," said Benny.

Mr. Pound stood up. "Well, I'd better be going," he said. "Thank you for the tea."

When he had left, Mrs. Teague shook her head. "Poor Edgar. I'm afraid the loss of the diamond has upset him. He's not himself. In fact, I think he looks worse tonight than on the evening of the theft."

"He was acting kind of weird," said Henry.

"Well, we'll find the diamond and then he'll feel better," said Benny.

"I hope you're right, Benny," said Jessie. "I hope you're right."

CHAPTER 8

The Chase

The next morning, Jessie leaned on the railing of the balcony and peered down. People scurried by on the street below. She sighed. "Too many people," she muttered.

"Too many people? In New York?" teased Henry, who was sitting in a chair nearby. At the small table, Violet was reading the newspaper to Benny.

"Read it again," said Benny. "About the diamond."

"It just says there are no new clues, Benny," Violet said.

"And too many suspects," said Jessie. "That's what I meant."

Violet and Benny looked up. "Too many?"

"Lydia, Mr. Evans, Mr. Saunders, Mr. Leed," said Jessie. "Or Lydia and Mr. Saunders working together, or Lydia and Mr. Evans, or Mr. Evans and Mr. Saunders."

"That's a lot of possibilities," agreed Henry.

"Seven," said Benny, who'd been counting on his fingers. "And Mr. Pound. Eight."

"Okay. And Mr. Pound," said Jessie. "Maybe he *did* have something to do with it."

"Eight," said Benny. "And Mr. Pound and Lydia. And Mr. Pound and Mr. Evans. And Mr. Pound and Mr. Saunders. Eleven ways the diamond could have been taken in all."

At that moment, the phone rang. It was Mr. Leed, saying that Mr. Evans was on his way up to the apartment.

"You're early today," said Mrs. Teague when she let Mr. Evans in.

"I woke up early," said Mr. Evans. "And

I believe an electrician should go with the current. That's a joke."

Mrs. Teague smiled.

"Anyway, I've got work to do," said Mr. Evans.

"We have work to do, too," said Henry.

"Are you going to look for clues to the mystery of the missing diamond?" asked Grandfather.

Mr. Evans looked up. "I saw a picture of it in the newspaper. Nice-looking little gem. Gave me a real charge. That's a joke."

"Oh," said Jessie. She looked at her watch. "Well, we'd better go."

Quickly the Aldens helped clear away the breakfast dishes and clean up. Then they hurried out the door.

They reached the sidewalk in front of the building just in time to see Lydia Critt hurrying down the street. She was wearing jeans and a green sweatshirt that said CRITT'S CRITTERS, and was carrying a very large backpack.

"Come on!" said Jessie. They raced after Lydia.

Today, Lydia walked into one of the big hotels at the bottom of the park. The Aldens followed her in. People with suitcases and briefcases filled the lobby. The children saw Lydia vanish down a hallway. But when they reached the hallway, she was gone.

"She must have gone into the bathroom," said Jessie.

"There's no door at the end of the hall," said Henry. "She'll have to come back out the way she came in. We'll wait in the lobby."

The Aldens found the perfect seat, on a small sofa in the corner behind a potted plant. They took turns peering out between its leaves.

Lydia was gone for a long time. When she came back out into the lobby, they saw why. They almost didn't recognize her.

She had completely changed clothes. She was wearing a dress, high heels, a big hat with a flower on it, and she had on gloves. The only thing that was the same was the backpack she was carrying. Earrings flashed at her earlobes, and Violet gave a little gasp when she saw the twinkle of light at Lydia's throat.

"The diamond?" she gasped.

"No," Henry whispered. "It's the crystal she always wears."

"Why did she change clothes?" Jessie wanted to know. "Do you think she knew we were following her and is trying to throw us off?"

"Maybe," said Henry.

"We'll have to be extra careful now," said Benny.

This time, when they followed Lydia out onto the street, they crossed to the other side.

And this time, Lydia kept stopping to look back. Every time she did, the Aldens pretended to be shopping, staring into the store windows.

"She *does* know we're following her," said Violet.

Suddenly Lydia threw up her hand and jumped out into the street. A yellow car swerved toward her.

Violet clamped her hands over her eyes.

"Oh, no!" cried Jessie, springing forward. "That car is going to hit Lydia!"

But it didn't. It screeched to a stop right beside her and the Aldens realized that the yellow car was a taxicab.

As the door of the cab slammed, Jessie jumped to the curb and threw up her hand.

"Jessie! What are you doing?" asked Henry.

Another yellow cab screeched to the curb and stopped.

"Get in!" Jessie panted. Then she leaned forward and said to the driver, "Follow that cab!"

They sped through the streets of Manhattan so quickly that the stores and people lining the sidewalks blurred as they went by. Then the cab turned and turned again. Now the streets were lined with theaters.

"Times Square," said Henry. "Broadway and the Theater District."

Ahead of them, Lydia's cab pulled to the curb.

"Stop here," Jessie said. "At the corner."

Quickly they paid the driver and got out just as Lydia hurried across the sidewalk. She stopped at a door and touched the crystal at her throat.

"For luck," whispered Violet almost to herself.

Then Lydia took a deep breath, opened the door, and disappeared inside.

The Aldens raced up to the door and stopped.

Then Henry read the sign posted on the door. " 'Auditions today for *Diamonds and Hearts*. A new mystery about stolen jewels . . . and love.' "

Then Henry began to laugh.

"What's so funny?" Benny said.

"She isn't a thief," said Henry, laughing harder. "She's an actress!"

Now Violet was smiling. "That's why she put on those funny clothes, isn't it?" she asked.

"Why?" asked Benny.

"Of course! Because she was going to an audition," said Jessie.

"What's an audition?" asked Benny. By now he was *very* confused.

"You remember when we were in that play, Benny. An audition is when you try out for a part in a show," explained Violet.

"Oh. So she wasn't in disguise. She was dressed up for the play," said Benny.

"Right, Benny," said Henry.

"And that's why she was in Tiffany's!" Jessie exclaimed suddenly. "What better place to do research about a play called *Diamonds and Hearts*? She was studying the way the other people were dressed in Tiffany's, too. That's how she is dressed today — like some of those people at Tiffany's."

"With her crystal necklace for a diamond," said Benny.

"You're right," said Henry.

"Does that mean she's not the thief?" asked Benny. He sounded a little relieved.

"Well, she could still be a thief," said Jessie. "But somehow, I don't think so. I think she's too busy to be a thief!"

Henry had managed to stop laughing. "Well, we might as well walk back to Mrs. Teague's," he said.

As they walked back uptown, they talked about the mystery.

"I'm glad it's not Lydia," said Benny. "I like her. And so does Watch. Because she likes dogs."

"Me, too," admitted Jessie.

"But if it isn't Lydia, who is it?" asked Violet.

"Maybe Mr. Pound did it," said Benny suddenly. "Maybe he's just pretending the diamond is stolen."

"Maybe, Benny," said Henry. "But remember, he'd have to know an awful lot about alarm systems."

"That's true," said Benny.

Violet said, "What about Mr. Saunders, the doorman? He could have let someone in without making them sign in."

"That's true, too," agreed Jessie. "I definitely think we should keep Mr. Saunders as a suspect."

"Don't forget Mr. Evans," said Henry.

"Why Mr. Evans?" asked Violet.

"Because he's an electrician. He could probably figure out how to tamper with an alarm so that no one could tell," said Henry.

"Do you think he broke into Mr. Pound's apartment and took the diamond?" asked Benny.

"But the lock on the door of Mr. Pound's apartment hadn't been broken," objected Henry. "The police said so."

"Maybe we should ask Lydia," said Benny.

"Ask Lydia what?" said Jessie, puzzled.

"About diamonds," said Benny. "She's in a play about stolen diamonds. And she has a lucky diamond necklace. . . . I mean, a *crystal* necklace."

Jessie stared at Benny. And then her mouth dropped open. "That's it, Benny! That's it!"

CHAPTER 9

No Joke

"What?" said Benny.

"Remember what you said, Benny?" said Jessie. "About Lydia's crystal necklace?"

"The one like a diamond?" asked Benny.

"Yes!" cried Jessie. "The crystal that Lydia wears for luck is like a diamond. Think, Benny. Where else have we seen crystals like diamonds? Lots of them."

Benny frowned.

Violet gasped. "The chandelier!"

Henry said, "You're right. Mrs. Teague's

chandelier. But what does that have to do with anything?"

"Because I think the Elizabeth Star is hidden there. And all we have to do to catch the thief is find out who hid it," said Jessie.

"In the chandelier?" asked Benny. "The diamond is hidden in the chandelier?"

"Yes," said Jessie.

"Let's go!" cried Henry.

They raced back to Mrs. Teague's apartment and ran past Mr. Leed.

"Where's the fire?" asked Mr. Leed, startled, as they ran by.

"No fire," Henry managed to say. "Diamonds."

The elevator seemed to take forever to get down to the lobby. Suddenly Henry pointed at the stairs. "Come on. That'll be faster," he said.

They began to run up the long flights of stairs. By the time they reached the ninth floor, they were all gasping for breath. As they burst into the hall, they heard the elevator doors closing.

But they didn't stop. They ran to Mrs. Teague's apartment.

Jessie led the way into the dining room. She pulled out a chair and jumped up on it. "It's not there," she said.

"Jessie? What's wrong?" asked Mrs. Teague, coming out of her study down the hall.

Then she said, "Doesn't the chandelier look nice? Mr. Evans noticed how dusty it had gotten and gave it a good cleaning."

"Mr. Evans? Where is he?" Violet looked around wildly.

"He just this second left. I'm surprised you didn't see him in the hall," began Mrs. Teague.

"The elevator!" exclaimed Henry.

Jessie jumped from the chair and, without waiting to give Mrs. Teague an explanation, the children raced out of the apartment.

This time they ran down the stairs so fast that Benny felt dizzy.

"Mr. Evans!" cried Jessie as they burst into the lobby. "Where is he?"

"He just left," said Mr. Leed.

"Which way did he go?" asked Henry.

"Turned left. He might have parked his truck around the corner. You can't park out front, you know. That's for taxis and — "

They didn't wait to hear the rest. They raced out of the building and down the sidewalk. Feet pounding the cement, they ran around the corner.

"There!" Jessie pointed.

A blue truck with the words EVANS' ELEC-TRIC painted on the side was parked just up ahead and Mr. Evans was walking toward it with his car keys in his hand.

Henry didn't hesitate. He ran and jumped right in front of the driver's-side door. Violet, Benny, and Jessie ran and stood behind Mr. Evans so he couldn't escape.

Mr. Evans put his hands on his hips. "Hey. What's going on?" he demanded.

"I think you know," said Jessie. She held out her hand. "The diamond, please."

"Diamond? What diamond? I don't know what you're talking about." Mr. Evans raised his voice. "Move!" he called to Henry.

Henry folded his arms and shook his head.

"You have the Elizabeth Star," said Jessie. "We know you do."

"Ha!" said Mr. Evans. "Very funny. Get out of my way or I'll call the police."

"Call them," said Jessie. "And tell them how you took the Elizabeth Star from its hiding place in Mrs. Teague's chandelier."

Mr. Evans dropped his arms to his sides. There was a long silence.

"No police," he said.

"Where's the diamond?" Benny asked.

Slowly, Mr. Evans reached into his shirt pocket and took out an old piece of cloth spattered with paint. He unwrapped it and held it out. There in his hand glittered the Elizabeth Star.

"I knew it," breathed Jessie.

"You stole it!" Benny said. "You stole the Elizabeth Star."

"No!" cried Mr. Evans. "I didn't."

"Then how did you know it was there?"

asked Violet. She sneezed, and stepped back a little.

"I was working up on the ladder yesterday morning and I saw it. But there was no way I could get to it without arousing suspicion. Mrs. Teague or Mr. Alden or someone was always around. Anyway, I figured it was safe and I could leave it there until I finished work."

"You didn't steal it and put it there?" asked Jessie.

"No!" said Mr. Evans. "But seeing it there gave me quite a shock, I can tell you." He managed a feeble smile. "And that's no joke."

Violet sneezed again and said, "You make me sneeze. It's the dust."

Mr. Evans gave her a puzzled look.

"It was you," said Violet. "You're the one who locked us in the secret room. And you left dust all over Mr. Pound's apartment."

"Yeah, well, I didn't mean to hurt you. Just scare you a little. Keep you from figuring out where the diamond was until I could get it safely away from Mrs. Teague's apartment," said Mr. Evans.

"Well, it didn't scare us. Not one bit," declared Benny.

"Mr. Saunders didn't tell you to go up and scare us?" asked Violet.

"No," said Henry, before Mr. Evans could answer.

"No," said Mr. Evans. "What has Mr. Saunders got to do with anything?"

"No. No, I don't think it was Mr. Saunders. And I don't think it was Lydia," Henry went on.

"I don't know what you're talking about now," complained Mr. Evans.

"Me either," said Benny.

"I think I know who took the diamond and hid it in the chandelier. Now all we have to do is set a trap and catch the thief . . . with your help, Mr. Evans," Henry added.

"Help you?" said Mr. Evans.

"Yes," said Henry. "And if you do, maybe the police will go easier on you."

"Plug me in," said Mr. Evans. His smile

was a little more genuine now. "That was a joke."

"Mr. Pound, come in," said Mrs. Teague.

"What's this? The children visiting you have actually found the diamond?" said Mr. Pound. Out came his handkerchief. He mopped his face.

"Did I say that when I called? I'm sorry. I should have said they found some new clues," said Mrs. Teague.

"Oh," said Mr. Pound. He sounded relieved. "Where are they?"

"They had to go to the store to get some more dog food for Watch," said Mrs. Teague. "Their grandfather went with them. I'm here by myself, except for Mr. Evans, at the moment."

"Mr. Evans?" asked Mr. Pound.

"The electrician. But he's out drinking a cup of coffee in the kitchen," said Mrs. Teague.

Crouched behind the kitchen door, Violet whispered, "Do you think he believes Mrs. Teague?"

"Shhh," warned Jessie.

"Shhh," Benny said to Watch, tightening his hold on the dog's collar.

"Why don't you sit in the dining room and . . . Oh, dear, I hear the phone ringing in my study. You just sit right here and I'll be right back." Mrs. Teague pulled out a chair, nodded at Mr. Pound, and hurried out of the dining room.

She was barely out of sight down the hall before Mr. Pound jumped to his feet. He climbed onto the chair and stretched his arm up toward the chandelier. He frowned. He leaned sideways and peered at the rows of dangling crystals.

"It's got to be here," he muttered.

"Now," said Jessie.

Mr. Evans pushed open the kitchen door and walked into the dining room, letting the door almost close behind him. He looked up at Mr. Pound. Mr. Pound looked down at him.

"Looking for something?" said Mr. Evans.

"I, er . . . well," said Mr. Pound.

"You know," said Mr. Evans, "I'm an

electrician, and while I was wiring the dining room, I noticed something very interesting about that chandelier."

"What?" said Mr. Pound.

"This," said Mr. Evans, pulling the Elizabeth Star out of his pocket.

"That's the Elizabeth Star," said Mr. Pound. He grew very pale.

"I wondered how it got up there," said Mr. Evans.

"That's mine," said Mr. Pound, getting down off the chair. "You must give it to me."

"I think I should give it to the police. Maybe there's a reward," said Mr. Evans.

Mr. Pound took out his handkerchief and wiped his face. He looked ill. "No need to do that," he said. "Yes, I hid the Star. And I'd like it to stay hidden. I couldn't bear to lose it."

"Go on," said Mr. Evans.

"So maybe we could make a deal," said Mr. Pound.

"And maybe not," said Henry, pushing open the kitchen door.

CHAPTER 10

A Thief's Regret

"You!" Mr. Pound staggered back as the children came out of the kitchen and Mrs. Teague and Grandfather Alden came in from the living room. "What are you doing here?"

"Catching a thief," said Jessie. "A thief who stole from himself."

Mr. Pound looked around wildly. For a moment, it seemed as if he might try to run out the door. Watch growled a little under his breath.

Then Mr. Pound collapsed onto the

chair. "It's true. It's all true. I'm sorry I deceived you all. My company . . . it's in trouble. I thought if the Elizabeth Star disappeared, I could collect the insurance. And I would still get to keep it. It was my wife's. It's all I have left of her. I couldn't bear to let it go."

"That was wrong," said Benny.

"I know," said Mr. Pound.

"No one tampered with the alarm," said Henry. "You must have punched in the right code to open the door, then reset it and punched in the wrong code. That's why the alarm went off."

Mr. Pound nodded. "And then I broke the glass case and took the diamond. The sound of the alarm covered the sound of the breaking glass and no one noticed what I was doing in all the confusion."

"Where did you hide it?" asked Violet.

Mr. Pound held up his handkerchief. "In here. I wrapped the handkerchief around my hand to break the glass. Then I wrapped the star inside the handkerchief."

"And then, when you were downstairs,

you hid the diamond in the chandelier," said Jessie.

"Yes. I thought of that at dinner. It seemed like a brilliant idea at the time. I had no idea how hard it would be to get the diamond back. . . ." His voice trailed off.

"That's why you kept sitting in the dining room the other day," said Benny. "You were going to take the diamond back. But *I* stopped you."

"Yes, you did," said Mr. Pound. He sighed heavily. "I didn't mean to do this. I had been planning to sell the Elizabeth Star to save my business, but the thought of losing it made me so terribly sad. It was Kathryn's, you see. It's all I have left of her."

Mr. Pound stared into space a moment before he went on. "But after I met you children in the elevator and invited you to come see the Star, the idea came to me: If I could fool the police into thinking the Star was stolen, I could save my business with the insurance payment and still keep the Star. I thought you'd be the perfect witnesses. After all, you were just children. You wouldn't notice what was really going on."

"But we did," said Jessie.

"Because we're children *and* detectives," said Benny. "Very good detectives."

"That's true," said Mrs. Teague. "If you'd asked me, I could have told you. After all, I was there when the Aldens solved the mystery at the dog show."

"Mr. Pound," Violet said softly, "may I ask you something?"

"Of course, Violet. I owe you that at least."

"You tried to keep the Star hidden and all to yourself, but didn't you tell us your wife wanted people to see it? That she wanted to share it?"

"That's very true, Violet."

"Well, I know a place where lots of people would see it — the Museum of Natural History, with the other beautiful gems."

"And there are lots of kids there," said Benny. "Mrs. Teague told us you liked children."

Mrs. Teague looked embarrassed, but Benny went right on talking. "And the museum's so close you could visit the Elizabeth Star whenever you wanted to and you could see all those children, too."

Mr. Evans put the diamond on the table in front of Mr. Pound. Mr. Pound looked at the Elizabeth Star for some time, then looked up at Mr. Evans. "I guess we'd both better talk to the police," he said.

"I think it would be the right thing to do," said Henry.

"I think if you confess," Grandfather put in, "you'll be able to work something out so you don't go to jail. After all, you haven't yet actually reported it missing to your insurance company, have you?"

Mr. Pound shook his head. "No, I haven't."

Grandfather went on, "And Mr. Evans here did cooperate, finally. If *you* don't press charges against him perhaps the police will drop the case. . . ."

When Mr. Pound had left, Jessie said to Mr. Evans, "Thanks for your help in solving the mystery."

"Glad to do it," said Mr. Evans. "An honest electrician, that's me." He emphasized the word *honest* and added, "From now on."

"Good," said Violet, smiling at him.

"Hey, I saw the light," said Mr. Evans. "That's a joke."

"In the chandelier?" asked Benny, puzzled.

Everyone laughed. And, as usual, Benny laughed, too, although he wasn't quite sure why everyone was laughing.

The Aldens spent their last day in New York City hunting for souvenirs and packing. By late afternoon they were waiting in the lobby with Mrs. Teague for the hired car that would take them to the train station when the elevator doors slid silently open.

"Look out," cried a familiar voice. And out came Lydia into the hall. But this time, she didn't have five French bulldogs on a leash. She had a huge Irish wolfhound.

"Woof," said Watch, and stopped, unsure of himself. Even he had never seen a dog that big.

"Don't worry. Erin — that's her name — is very friendly," said Lydia, pulling on the leash.

Erin sat down.

"Is Erin one of your new dog clients?" asked Violet.

"Yep. And guess what? I just got a part in a new play. *Diamonds and Hearts*. On Broadway!" said Lydia.

"Congratulations," all the Aldens said at once.

"You'll have to come see it. It opens at Christmas. And you know why I got the part?" she went on.

"Your lucky crystal?" asked Henry.

"Well, that, maybe. And the dog who has a starring role liked me!" Lydia beamed. "I guess it's all my experience with dogs. Critt's Critters is going to make me a star!"

Erin stood up.

"Okay," Lydia said to Erin.

"Lydia," said Jessie quickly, "a few nights ago, after you walked the French bulldogs, you stayed upstairs a long time. What happened?"

Lydia thought a moment, then grinned. "Jill got away, out in the hall. It took me almost twenty minutes to catch her, the little rascal."

"Another mystery solved," said Jessie, grinning.

"Speaking of mysteries," said Lydia, "did you hear about Mr. Pound? It's in all the papers. His stolen diamond was found and he's going to donate it to the Museum of Natural History. Can you imagine giving such a valuable thing away? I bet there's a story behind *that* news item!"

"I bet there is," said Henry, and the children exchanged smiles.

At that moment, Lydia noticed the luggage for the first time. "You're leaving?" she said.

"It's time to go home," Grandfather Alden said.

Mr. Saunders came in. "Your car is ready," he said.

"Come back soooon," Lydia said as Erin the wolfhound pulled her through the door.

"Yes, come back soon," said Mrs. Teague. She hugged everybody, even Watch.

And Mr. Saunders actually waved as the hired car pulled away from the building.

Violet sighed as she looked out of the window of the train. The lights of New York City stretched across the skyline.

"Like diamonds," said Benny, looking out over her shoulder.

"We had fun, didn't we?" said Henry.

"Yes," said Violet. "I hope we come back."

Grandfather, who was sitting across the aisle, heard Violet. "I guess New York doesn't seem so big now, does it, Violet?"

"It's still big," said Violet. "But most of the people are pretty nice."

"Don't worry," said Benny. "We'll be back. There are about a million mysteries in a big city like New York. And somebody's got to solve them."

Violet smiled. "Who else? The Alden Family Detective Agency, of course."

THE WINDY CITY MYSTERY

created by

GERTRUDE CHANDLER WARNER

Illustrated by Charles Tang

No part of this publication may be reproduced in whole or in part, or stored in a retrieval system, or transmitted in any form, or by any means, electronic, mechanical, photocopying, recording, or otherwise, without written permission of the publisher. For information regarding permission, write to Albert Whitman & Company, 6340 Oakton Street, Morton Grove, IL 60053-2723.

ISBN 0-8075-5448-0

Copyright © 1998 by Albert Whitman & Company. All rights reserved. Published simultaneously in Canada by General Publishing, Limited, Toronto. THE BOXCAR CHILDREN is a registered trademark of Albert Whitman & Company.

7 9 10 8 6

Printed in the U.S.A.

Contents

CHAPTER   PAGE

1. The Windy City   1
2. A New Mystery   13
3. No Clue   24
4. Another Clue   34
5. Two Lions and Tiny Rooms   46
6. Picture, Picture   56
7. Old Stories and New Fire Engines   67
8. The Final Clue   78
9. Another Phone Call   88
10. X Marks the Spot   100
11. Buried Treasure   109
     Greetings from Chicago! Activities   122

CHAPTER 1

The Windy City

"Look for Chad," Grandfather Alden said.

He and the Alden children had just gotten off an airplane.

"We've never met Chad," Henry, who was fourteen, reminded him.

Grandfather smiled. "That's right," he said. "I forgot."

Twelve-year-old Jessie glanced around the airport. "What does he look like?"

"I haven't seen him in a long time,"

Grandfather answered. "I'm not sure I'd recognize him myself."

"There he is!" Benny said. He skipped toward a tall, thin young man.

The others followed.

"Welcome to Chicago," the young man said.

"Chad Piper!" Mr. Alden said. "You've grown up!" He introduced Chad to the Alden children.

Then Jessie said, "Benny, how did you know this was Chad?"

Chad held up a sign. It read ALDENS.

"I'm six!" Benny said. "I can read!"

"I wasn't sure I'd recognize you," Chad said, leading the group down the long hall. "So I made the sign."

Ten-year-old Violet thought it would be fun to spend the day just watching the people come and go. "This place is really big," she said.

"O'Hare is one of the largest and busiest airports in the world," Chad told her.

They picked up their luggage from the carousel and went to the parking garage.

When they were settled in the car and on their way, Chad asked the children, "Have you decided what you want to see?"

"They didn't have much time to plan," Mr. Alden said.

"Grandfather just told us about the trip two days ago," Henry added.

"No problem," Chad said. "I'm to be your guide when your grandfather and my father are busy."

Jacob Piper, Chad's father, owned Piper Paper Products. Mr. Alden, who owned a mill, had come to see him on business.

"We'll pick up some maps and brochures tomorrow," Chad continued. "Then you can decide what you want to see."

"Oh, look!" Violet exclaimed.

Ahead, the city skyline was golden in the late afternoon sun.

"There it is," Chad said. "The Windy City."

"Wow!" Benny said, pointing to a building that towered over all the others. "That building looks like a giant!"

"It's the Sears Tower," Chad told them.

"One hundred and ten stories high — counting the antennae on top. It's the tallest building in North America."

Before long, they turned off the expressway onto city streets. People hurried along the sidewalks and in and out of buildings.

Chad parked the car. "Here we are," he said.

Everyone got out. Henry helped Chad with the suitcases.

Benny tipped his head back to look up. This building was not one hundred and ten stories, but it was tall. "Is this where we're staying?" he asked.

Chad nodded. "Piper Paper Products owns an apartment here. My father keeps it for visitors."

Inside, a man in a blue uniform was talking on a phone.

Chad gave Mr. Alden a key. "Take the elevator to twenty," he said. "Apartment 2004. I'll be up in a few minutes."

As the Aldens entered the elevator, Violet glanced over her shoulder. "Chad's talking to the man in the uniform," she said.

Henry turned around to look. "That's the doorman."

Upstairs, Benny ran ahead, reading the numbers on the doors. "Here it is!" he said.

Mr. Alden unlocked the door and stepped back to let the children enter. The apartment had high ceilings and lots of woodwork.

On their right was a small kitchen. Benny went to the refrigerator. He opened it and peered inside. "Look at all this food!" he said. "Eggs and bacon and jam and milk and soda and . . . everything!" He closed the door. "I'm going to like it here."

Beyond the kitchen was a large living room. Violet crossed to the wall of windows.

Grandfather followed her. "There's Lake Michigan," he said.

A few blocks east, the lake sparkled.

"It's beautiful," Violet said.

Henry came up beside them. "It sure is," he agreed.

Jessie came into the room. "There are three big bedrooms," she told them.

"Grandfather can have one. Henry, you and Benny can have another, and Violet and I will take the third."

The other Aldens took their suitcases and followed her. Jessie was good at organizing things.

They were in their separate bedrooms when Chad came into the apartment and called, "Where is everyone?"

The Aldens returned to the living room.

"This is a nice place," Jessie said.

Chad grinned. "I'm glad you like it. I helped decorate it. It's a challenge — an old place like this."

"Are you a decorator?" Violet asked.

Chad shook his head. "Actually, I work part-time for my father," he said, "but I am going to school. I want to be an artist."

"Violet's an artist." There was pride in Benny's voice.

"Are you?" Chad said. "That's great!"

Violet blushed. "I'm not really an artist," she objected. "I just like to sketch."

"That's how I started," Chad told her. "I'd like to see your work."

"You brought your sketchbook, didn't you?" Henry asked.

Violet nodded. She always packed her sketchbook.

"Good," Chad said. "We'll make time to do some drawing." He turned to the others. "If everything's all right here, I'll let you get settled."

"Are we going to meet your father?" Henry asked.

Chad frowned. "I don't know. He's always busy with some new plan for his business. Thank goodness he has his hobby or he would never relax!"

Jessie wanted to ask what his father's hobby was, but Mr. Alden said, "I know you're busy. You run along. Tell your father I'll see him in the morning."

"And I'll be back bright and early to show you the city," Chad said to the children. He started out. At the door, he said, "Are there any questions about the apartment or anything?"

"I have a question," Benny piped up. "Can we eat anything we find?"

Chad laughed. "Anything," he said. "Just don't eat it all at once."

After Chad left, the Aldens unpacked.

When they had finished, Jessie said, "I have a surprise." She showed them a book about Chicago.

Grandfather Alden was more surprised than anyone. "That's my old school workbook. Where did you find it, Jessie?"

"In the bookcase at home," she answered.

"You used that book in *school*?" Benny said. He thought it must be very old, but he didn't say so.

"We were studying American cities," Grandfather said. He took the book from Jessie and glanced through it. "Soon after we finished our study, your great-grandfather brought me here on the train. Very few people traveled by airplane then."

"A train is still the best way to travel," Henry said, thinking of the boxcar he and his brother and sisters had lived in after their parents had died. When their grandfather found them, he brought the children and their boxcar to his home.

The others agreed with Henry. "You see so much more," Jessie concluded.

Grandfather closed the book. "This is a very old book," he said. "You will find things have changed."

The children sat down to study the book.

"Chicago's a terrific city," Mr. Alden put in. "It was a good city before the fire and a great one after."

"Fire?" Violet repeated.

Henry held up the workbook. "It tells about it in here," he told his sister. "It's called the Great Chicago Fire. It nearly destroyed the whole city way back in 1871." He showed the other Aldens a picture of a building. "That's the Water Tower — one of the few buildings that wasn't burned."

"How did the fire start?" Violet asked.

Henry studied the book. Then he said, "No one knows."

"The most popular explanation concerns a cow and a lantern," Grandfather said.

"That story is here in the book," Henry said. "People thought Mrs. O'Leary's cow kicked over a lantern and started the fire. High winds spread it."

"Is that why they call it the Windy City?" Benny asked. "Because of the winds?"

"Could be," Grandfather answered. "But most say it's because residents bragged so much about their city. People said they were windy — full of hot air."

Jessie said, "This city is full of mysteries!"

Grandfather agreed. "Those mysteries will never be solved," he said. "But here's one you can solve: Shall we eat supper here or go out?"

"Here!" the younger Aldens all said.

Grandfather started for the kitchen. "I'll be the cook tonight."

The children looked at one another. Grandfather seldom did the cooking.

"Do you want some help?" Jessie asked.

"You can set the table," Grandfather answered.

They decided to move the table nearer to the windows. Then Jessie and Violet poked through drawers until they found a table-cloth and silverware. Henry and Benny found the dishes.

"Oh, look," Benny said. "A pink mug!" It reminded him of the cracked pink cup he had used when they lived in the boxcar. "That'll be my cup," he said.

Before long, Grandfather announced, "Dinner's ready."

He brought five omelettes to the table.

"They look delicious," Violet said.

Benny took a taste. "Ummm. It *is* delicious!"

"You didn't know your old grandfather was such a good cook, did you?"

"All the Aldens are good cooks," Henry said.

"But how did you do it so fast?" Jessie asked.

"Ahh," Mr. Alden answered. "There's a mystery for you."

Benny poured milk into the pink mug. "That's our mystery for this trip," he said. "There won't be any more."

Grandfather tilted his head to one side. His eyes twinkled. "Don't be too sure of that, Benny. You children seem to attract mysteries."

CHAPTER 2

A New Mystery

Henry was the first one up in the morning. He made bacon and eggs and poured orange juice.

Benny came into the kitchen rubbing his eyes. "I smell bacon," he said.

Soon the others were up, too. Violet made toast. Jessie made coffee for Grandfather.

When he joined them in the living room, Mr. Alden said, "That's what I like to see: teamwork."

They sat before the large windows where

they watched the early sun trace golden paths across the lake.

"I wonder what we'll do today," Jessie said.

"Just be sure to wear comfortable shoes," Grandfather told them. "I'm sure you'll do a lot of walking."

The telephone rang. "Chad will be late," Grandfather said as he hung up.

"That's all right, Grandfather," Jessie said. "We aren't ready anyway."

Mr. Alden looked at his watch. "I have a meeting at Piper's office. I don't like to keep everyone waiting."

"You can go, Grandfather," Henry said. "We'll be fine."

"I'm sure you will be," Mr. Alden said. "I sometimes forget how responsible you are." He looked at his watch again. "Chad said he'd meet you downstairs in the lobby. We'll go downstairs together."

"Hurry up and get ready," Jessie directed. "We'll do the dishes later."

They were dressed and ready in a flash. In the elevator, Mr. Alden gave Henry the apartment key. "In case you get back before I do," he explained. "I'm sure Cob has another key. I'll get one from him."

"Who's Cob?" Benny asked.

"Mr. Piper. His real name is *Jacob*, but everyone calls him *Cob*."

"Cob Piper," Benny said. He liked the sound of it.

Downstairs, the doorman was talking to someone — a balding man with a bushy mustache. Wearing bib overalls and carrying a striped cap, he looked out of place. When he saw the Aldens, he hurried away. The doorman followed him out of the building.

Grandfather looked at his watch. "I have to go," he said. "Are you sure you'll be all right?"

"Of course, Grandfather," Henry said. "We'll be fine."

"Well, then, I'll be on my way," Mr. Alden said. "Have fun, and don't wander off without Chad. This is a big city."

The Aldens sat down on a marble bench.

"Did Grandfather seem like he was acting a little strange to you?" Jessie asked.

Henry nodded.

"He was probably just afraid he was going to be late for his meeting," Violet said.

Henry nodded. "Grandfather likes to be on time."

They fell silent, watching the people hurrying through the lobby. Outside, the doorman smiled at everyone who passed through the doors.

After a while Violet said, "I wonder where all these people are going."

"Most of them are probably headed to work," Henry said.

"What about that man with the big mustache?" Benny asked.

"He was dressed in overalls," Violet said. "I'll bet he doesn't work in an office."

"The city is full of all kinds of jobs," Jessie said.

"He looked like a railroad engineer," Henry added.

Just then they saw Chad outside. He stopped to talk to the doorman.

"Let's go." Henry stood up and started for the door.

"He's going away!" Benny observed as Chad hurried out of sight.

The doorman came in. "You must be the Aldens," he said, smiling. "I'm Willard. I have a message for you."

"From Chad?" Henry asked.

Willard nodded. "He says he'll be with you shortly. He had an errand down the street." He started away. "Oh, I almost forgot," he said, turning back. "This is for you, too." He handed Henry an envelope and went back outside.

"Who's that from?" Benny asked.

Henry studied the envelope. "It doesn't say."

"It's probably from Chad," Violet decided.

Henry opened the envelope and took out a piece of paper. "This is odd," he said, and he began to read the note aloud.

> *In this city*
> *There's lots to do.*
> *Follow my lead*
> *To each new clue.*

And when you've seen
All the rest,
You'll find the treasure
That is best.
NOTE WELL: DON'T TELL!

"Don't tell *what*, Henry?" Benny asked.

Henry shrugged. "I don't know. About the note, maybe, or . . . There's a clue on the bottom. Maybe that's it."

"A clue? What kind of clue?" Jessie said.

Henry read on:

CLUE #1
Find a structure
Straight and tall
Standing there
Through fire and all.

They drifted back to the bench and sat down. They were full of questions. *What did this note mean? Who had written it? Why was it given to them? What was the special treasure the note mentioned?*

"Chad wrote the note," Jessie decided.

"But why?" Henry wondered.

"Let's ask him," Benny said.

"The note says, 'Don't tell,' " Violet reminded him.

Benny was puzzled. "But if Chad wrote it, he already knows about it."

"You're right, Benny," Henry said, "but if he *did* write it, he doesn't want us to know he did."

"It's some kind of game — a treasure hunt," Jessie said. "We should just go along with it."

"Then we'd better figure out the clue," Henry concluded. He reread it.

"A *structure* — is that a *building*?" Benny asked.

Henry nodded. "It could be a building. But there are other kinds of structures."

"Let's say it's a building, Henry," Jessie suggested.

"Okay. A building — straight and tall —"

"There's Chad!" Benny said.

This time Chad came inside. "Sorry I'm late," he said. "I hope you weren't bored."

Henry stuffed the note into his pocket.

"Actually, we were busy . . . figuring things out," he said.

The Aldens all watched Chad. If he had written the note, he would know they had been trying to figure out the clue. His reaction would give him away.

Chad did not react. Instead, he said, "Let's get moving!" and sailed through the doors with the Aldens at his heels.

Chad led the way along the broad sidewalks. "I hope you like to walk," he said.

Benny looked at the tall buildings and the busy streets. "Where are we going?" he asked.

"To the Water Tower," Chad answered. "It's not far."

"What's at the Water Tower?" Violet asked.

"Long ago it contained instruments to measure water pumped from Lake Michigan. Now it's a visitors' center," Chad said. "We can get information and maps there."

"The Water Tower!" Benny said. "We saw a picture of it in Grandfather's workbook. It looks like a castle."

"That's the one," Chad said.

Henry remembered something else about the building. He caught Jessie's eye. They dropped back behind Chad.

"What is it, Henry?" Jessie asked.

"The Water Tower — it survived the fire!" he whispered.

Jessie nodded. " 'A structure/ Straight and tall.' "

" 'Standing there/ Through fire and all,' " Henry completed.

Was the Water Tower the answer to the riddle?

"It can't be the place," Jessie decided.

"Why?" Henry asked. "It fits the clue."

"But if Chad wrote the clue, he wouldn't just take us there, would he?" Jessie said. "He'd want us to figure it out for ourselves."

That was true, Henry agreed. Why would Chad lead them to this place after he had gone to the trouble of writing the clue? He couldn't think of a single reason.

Finally he said, "Maybe he didn't write it."

"Then who did?"

"Jessie! Henry!" Benny called excitedly. "Hurry up!"

"We'll talk about this later," Henry said, and he and Jessie caught up to the others.

Just ahead, looking like some kind of fairy castle, was the Water Tower.

"No wonder it survived the fire," Henry said. "It's made of stone."

They went inside.

"Oh, look at the floor!" Violet exclaimed.

Blues, greens, purples, and yellows in flowing patterns glittered beneath their feet.

"Beautiful, isn't it?" Chad said.

"What's it made of?" Henry asked.

"Broken glass and stones and shells."

"I guess you can make art out of anything," Benny said.

Chad laughed. "If you know what you're doing."

They gathered information from the racks along the walls.

"Henry," Jessie whispered. "Look for another clue."

Henry didn't need to be told. He was already looking.

CHAPTER 3

No Clue

"That should be enough," Chad said. He led them outside and found a bench. "Let's sit here and look through the brochures."

Jessie and Violet studied the leaflets. Benny looked at the colorful pictures. But Henry couldn't concentrate. He kept wondering about the clue. He was sure they had come to the right place: The Water Tower was certainly the solution to the puzzle. But where was the next clue? He stared up at the stone building. What secret was it keeping? He stood up and walked toward it.

"Where're you going, Henry?" Benny asked.

"To look at the building close up," he said. He ran his hand along the rough stone walls and glanced down at the ground. Seeing something, he picked it up. But it was only a paper scrap. He went back inside the Water Tower.

"Did you find anything, Henry?" It was Jessie. She had come inside after him.

He shook his head. "If this is the place, there has to be another clue."

But there was nothing out of place — nothing there to get the Aldens' attention.

"Maybe we're wrong," Jessie continued. "Maybe this isn't the place."

Violet was at the door. "Grandfather's here!"

They went back outside. Sure enough, Grandfather Alden was sitting beside Benny on the bench.

"Grandfather!" Jessie said. "What are you doing here?"

"Cob and I finished our business for the

day," Mr. Alden answered, "so I thought I'd join you."

"How did you know we'd be here?" Henry asked.

"Well, I . . . uh . . ." Grandfather didn't seem to have an answer. Finally he said, "Chad told me. Didn't you, Chad?"

Chad looked confused. "Did I? I don't remember telling you."

"You did say we'd pick up brochures and maps this morning," Jessie reminded him.

"That's right," Grandfather said. "And this is a visitors' center — just the place to do that." Changing the subject, he asked, "What are your plans for the day?"

"We're still deciding," Violet said.

"I have a suggestion," Mr. Alden said. "How about a baseball game? The Cubs are in town."

Benny jumped up and down. "Oh, good!" he said. "We can have lunch there!"

Grandfather stood up. "Chad, we'd like you to come along."

"Thanks, I'd love to go, but I have some schoolwork to do," Chad said. He added,

"I'll see you in the morning," and then he was gone.

"Jessie, I think you dropped something," Grandfather said.

Jessie looked behind her. Several pamphlets lay on the ground.

"I'll get them," Benny said.

Mr. Alden picked up a few leaflets that had blown some distance away. He handed them to Jessie. "Don't forget these."

She stacked the papers and put them in her backpack.

"How are we getting to the ballpark, Grandfather?" Violet asked.

"You'll see," Mr. Alden answered. "Just follow me."

Benny laughed. "You made a rhyme, Grandfather! Just like the —" Henry poked him. Then Benny remembered they were not supposed to tell anyone about the mystery.

They walked west. Two blocks away, Mr. Alden led them down a broad staircase.

"We're going to the subway," Henry observed.

"There's a lot happening underground in Chicago," Grandfather said.

Downstairs, Grandfather Alden paid the woman in the ticket booth and, single file, they pushed through the metal turnstile. More stairs took them to the station platform where tracks ran along both sides.

Grandfather said, "We want to go north."

Violet was the first to see the NORTH-BOUND sign.

Before long, a train screeched to a stop. Doors slid open. They all hopped on.

After several stops, the train began to climb. It emerged from the tunnel into the sun. Up, up went the tracks until they were high above the street. The train screeched past the buildings lining the way.

"What do you think of the El, Benny?" Grandfather asked.

"El?" Benny said.

Henry looked at Grandfather Alden. "Is that short for *elevated*?"

"Right you are, Henry," Mr. Alden answered.

Before long, a voice came over the public address system. "Wrigley Field, home of the Chicago Cubs!" it said.

The train squealed to a halt. The Aldens followed the crowd down the steep stairway.

"The game's going to be crowded," Benny decided.

And he was right. Still, there was plenty of room. They found good seats.

"Is anybody hungry?" Grandfather asked.

Benny raised his hand. "I am!"

Laughing, the others raised their hands, too.

"Give me your orders," Mr. Alden said. "Henry and I will go get lunch."

They all wanted hot dogs and peanuts.

"That's easy to remember," Henry said. He followed Grandfather out to the concession stands.

Jessie, Violet, and Benny watched the pregame action. All around them, people settled into seats, talking excitedly.

"Did you think more about the clue?" Violet asked Jessie.

"Henry and I thought the Water Tower was the place," Jessie answered.

"You're right," Violet said. "It fits the description."

Benny was surprised. "You mean we solved that clue, and I didn't even know it?"

"We're not sure we solved it," Jessie said.

Violet thought about that. Finally she asked, "If Chad wrote the clue, why didn't he let us figure it out?"

"But who else could have written it?" Benny asked.

"Henry and I asked both those questions, too," Jessie answered. "And another thing: There was no clue at the Water Tower. There has to be another clue. Where is it?"

Just then, Henry appeared, carrying a box of drinks. "Grandfather has the food," he said. He looked over his shoulder. Mr. Alden wasn't there. "That's funny. He was right behind me."

Benny got to his feet. "Let's go find him. I'm hungry." He and Henry trotted off.

"Where could he be?" asked Jessie.

"Look!" Violet said. "Up there!"

Jessie followed her sister's gaze.

High at the top of the bleachers, a man

wearing bib overalls and a cap took a seat.

"Isn't that the man we saw this morning?" Violet asked.

"It's hard to tell," Jessie answered.

"There's Grandfather!" Violet said. She stood up and waved.

"Where are Henry and Benny?" Grandfather asked as he approached.

"They went to look for you," Jessie told him.

Just then, the boys scampered down the stairs to join them.

"What happened to you, Grandfather?" Henry asked. "You were right behind me and then you . . . disappeared."

Grandfather handed the box of food to Jessie. "Sorry, I . . . uh . . . went back to get this." He pulled a cap out of his pocket and put it on Benny's head. It was blue. On the front was a red letter: C. "Now you're a real Cubs fan," he said.

Henry was puzzled. He had been with Grandfather when he bought the cap. Had Grandfather forgotten?

Benny passed out the food. "This smells so good," he said.

A voice boomed out over the field. "Plaaaaay ball!"

The teams took their positions.

The game began!

The crack of the bat, the shouts of the umpires, and the roar of the crowd soon pushed the mystery to the back of the Aldens' minds.

During the seventh inning, Grandfather Alden went for more peanuts. "Be right back," he said.

Watching him go, Violet saw someone else. "There's that man again," she said.

The man in the overalls hurried past. He was definitely the same man they had seen speaking with the doorman, yet he looked different somehow.

Benny giggled. "His mustache is crooked!" he said.

This time, Grandfather returned with the peanuts quickly. The Aldens enjoyed the rest of the game, and best of all, the Cubs won!

CHAPTER 4

Another Clue

Back at their apartment building, Willard opened the door for them. "How'd you like the ball game?" he asked. "When those Cubbies are good, they are really good."

Wide-eyed, Benny looked up at the man. "How'd you know we went to the game?"

Willard raised one eyebrow. "This is my building. I know all about the people in it."

The Aldens laughed — except Benny. He was wondering if Willard could be the man behind the mysterious clue.

Upstairs, Grandfather said, "I think I'll take a nap. All that rooting for the home team wore me out."

"You go ahead, Grandfather," Jessie said. "We'll do the breakfast dishes."

"If I'm not up, wake me in an hour," Mr. Alden said as he closed his bedroom door.

Violet helped with the dishes. "Next time, it's your turn," she said to her brothers.

After everything had been dried and put away, Jessie said, "We should decide where we want to go tomorrow with Chad." She took the brochures out of her backpack and laid them on the table.

Benny leaned in close to the others. "I think Willard wrote the clue," he whispered.

"Willard?" Henry said. "I doubt it."

Violet disagreed. "Benny might be right," she said. "Willard did give us the note, remember? And he never said it was from Chad."

"We didn't ask him," Henry said.

"That would explain why Chad took us to the Water Tower before we figured it out," Jessie said. "He didn't know about the clue."

"Willard did it," Benny said. "How else did he know we went to the ball game?"

Henry, Jessie, and Violet exchanged amused glances.

"Benny, you're the clue to that," Henry said.

Benny pointed to himself. "Me?"

Henry reached across the table and took the cap off Benny's head. "You're wearing a Cubs cap," he said.

Benny put the cap back on his head. "Oh, I forgot," he said.

Violet shuffled through the pamphlets. She held up a white envelope. "What's this?"

Jessie took it from her. "I don't know," she said. "There's no writing on it." Jessie opened it and took out a folded piece of paper. "It's another clue!" She read it aloud:

CLUE #2
When you hear
Two lions roar,
You are at
The proper door.
Go inside,
Walk around,
Find tiny rooms
On the ground.

Jessie looked up from the paper. "I must have gotten this at the Water Tower," she said.

"But I looked everywhere," Henry said. "There was nothing."

"You dropped some stuff, Jessie," Benny reminded her. "I picked it up. Maybe the clue was mixed in with that."

"Or it could have been with the things Grandfather picked up," Violet said.

Jessie reexamined the envelope. "But our name isn't on this," she said.

"Whoever put it there was sure we'd find it," Henry decided.

"Who knew we were going to be there?" Violet asked.

They could all answer that: Chad and Grandfather.

"Grandfather certainly didn't do it," Jessie said.

Henry nodded. "Chad's behind this."

"Or maybe Willard," Benny piped up. "He said he knows everything about the people in this building."

"We know one thing for sure," Violet said. "The Water Tower is definitely the answer to the first clue."

"How about this one?" Benny asked. "What's the answer to it?"

Jessie read the clue to them again. Then she sighed. "This one is really hard."

"Let's take it one line at a time," Henry suggested.

"The first is about lions roaring," Benny said.

"Zoos have lions," Violet put in.

"But do they have doors?" Jessie asked.

"Not the zoo itself," Henry said, "but the lion house would have doors."

"What about the little rooms?" Benny asked.

"*Tiny* rooms," Jessie corrected. "The clue says 'tiny rooms/ On the ground.' "

"Ants make tiny rooms," Benny said.

"Most of an anthill is *under* the ground," Henry said.

They heard Grandfather's voice in the bedroom. He was talking on the telephone.

Jessie piled the clue with the brochures and put them aside. "We'll get back to this later," she said.

Mr. Alden came into the room. "How about a picnic supper?"

Everyone thought that was a wonderful idea.

"Why don't you make sandwiches," he suggested. "I'll go downstairs to get a newspaper."

Jessie got out the bread, cold cuts, lettuce, and pickles. Benny got out the peanut butter and jelly. Violet took apples from the crisper and bananas from a bowl on the counter. Henry found paper plates and napkins.

"We can use my backpack to carry everything," Jessie said as she wrapped the last sandwich.

"Are there picnic tables where we're going?" Violet wondered aloud.

"We'll have to ask Grandfather," Henry said.

Benny went to the door and looked out into the hall. No Grandfather. "What's taking him so long?"

Mr. Alden *had* been gone a long time. Jessie wondered if something had happened to him. She did not want to alarm the others. "Let's look at the brochures while we wait," she said. "We haven't decided what we want to see tomorrow."

They had just sat down at the table when Grandfather came in.

"Where *were* you so long?" Benny asked.

Mr. Alden smiled. "I stopped to talk with Willard," he explained.

"We're ready to go," Violet told him.

"We'll need something to sit on." Grandfather looked around the apartment. In the hall closet, he found a blanket with a note taped to it. It said: FOR PICNICS.

"The Pipers thought of everything," Henry commented.

"Enjoy the concert," Willard said as they went out the door.

"We're going to a concert?" Violet asked. She loved music and played the violin.

"That we are," Mr. Alden answered.

"With a picnic supper?" Benny said. He couldn't imagine eating in a concert hall.

"This is a very special concert," Grandfather told him.

They walked along Michigan Avenue. Most of the shops and offices were closed now, but still the sidewalks were bustling with people.

Mr. Alden and Henry, who carried Jessie's backpack, were in the lead. Jessie, Violet, and Benny followed close behind. They approached a building fronted by a broad stairway.

"Look!" Benny said. "Lions!" He stopped abruptly.

Jessie and Violet stopped, too. They stared at the two large bronze lions on either side of the staircase. Each of the children was thinking the same thing: Could this building be the destination hinted at in Clue #2?

"We found it!" Benny said.

"But these lions don't roar," Jessie said.

"They *look* like they could," Benny answered.

Violet agreed. "They seem so real," she said. "I can almost hear them roar, too."

Thinking of the clue, Jessie said, "The place has doors."

"And an inside," Violet said.

"But what about the tiny rooms?" Benny asked.

Henry called to them.

"Coming!" Jessie responded. To Violet and Benny, she said, "We'll have to ask Chad about this building."

They followed Grandfather and Henry into Grant Park. Ahead were several rows of seats. Beyond those was a covered stage.

"A band shell," Violet said. "It's an outdoor concert!"

"It won't start for a while," Grandfather said. "We'll have our picnic while we wait."

They found a spot on the lawn and

spread out the blanket. Jessie began unpacking her backpack.

Grandfather pointed to a concession stand. "We can buy drinks here," he said. "Come on, Violet."

When they had gone, Jessie asked Henry, "Did you see those lions in front of that building?"

Henry nodded. "What about them?"

"The clue!" Benny said.

Henry's eyes opened wide. "Oh," he said. "I didn't think about that." He added, "But those lions — they aren't real."

Benny laughed. He imagined those two big greenish lions roaming the streets of Chicago. "I'm glad they're not," he said. He ran over to help carry the drinks.

Jessie handed the sandwiches around, and everyone took an apple or a banana.

It was a beautiful evening. They ate their supper and talked and joked. No thought of the mystery entered their minds.

The concert started just before dark. Benny lay back on the blanket. Before long, he was asleep.

The other Aldens listened to the music. "The blues," Grandfather called it.

Overhead, the sky was clear and star-filled. Surrounded by the music and the twinkling lights, the Aldens felt as though they were in a magical city.

But eventually the concert ended, and they joined the streams of people reluctantly leaving the park.

Rubbing his eyes, Benny asked, "Are we going home now?"

"There's just one more stop," Grandfather said, and he led them to a large fountain.

"This is Buckingham Fountain," Grandfather said. "It's a real treasure."

The word *treasure* reminded them of the mystery. Each of the Alden children thought about the same words in the first note: "And when you've seen/ All the rest,/ You'll find the treasure/ That is best." Everything they had seen that day was interesting. Each was a treasure in its own way. How would they ever know when they had discovered the best?

CHAPTER 5

Two Lions and Tiny Rooms

Chad arrived the next morning just as they were finishing breakfast. After the children told him what they had done the day before, Chad asked, "And what do you want to do today?"

Jessie held up the brochures. "These should help us decide," she said.

Grandfather came into the living room. He said, "Good morning, Chad." Adding, "See you later. I have a meeting with Cob Piper," he went out the door.

Chad thumbed through the pamphlets.

"Museums, historic places, theaters — you name it."

"Is there a zoo?" Henry asked.

"The Lincoln Park Zoo isn't too far," Chad answered. "We could take a bus."

"Do they have lions?" Benny asked.

Chad nodded. "Last time I was there, there were two," he answered.

The Aldens exchanged glances. *Two* lions! The zoo could be the answer to the second clue.

"How about tiny rooms?" Benny asked.

Chad looked puzzled. "Tiny rooms?"

Violet put a finger to her lips. Benny understood. He had almost told Chad about the clue. Jessie changed the subject. "We passed a building last night on the way to the concert," she said. "There were lions in front of it."

Chad beamed. "The Art Institute. I go to school there."

"We'd like to go there," Henry said.

"Great!" Chad responded. "I was going to suggest it. I thought Violet might be interested."

"We're all interested," Jessie said.

Henry stood up. "Let's go," he urged.

Downstairs, Willard held the doors for them. "So the Aldens are off on another adventure," he said. As they walked away, he called, "I hope you find what you're looking for."

Jessie whispered, "Did you hear that?"

All of the Aldens had heard it. Willard must know they were looking for the answer to the clue. If not, why would he say anything about finding what they were looking for?

Chad, who was a few steps ahead, stopped and turned. "Hear what?" he asked.

"Oh, nothing," Benny said. This time he remembered not to say anything that would give them away.

Then Henry surprised him by saying, "Willard said he hopes we find what we're looking for. We wonder what he means." He watched Chad closely. If he and Willard were in this together, he might give himself away.

Chad shrugged. "He means what he says.

You *are* looking for something, aren't you?"

Amazed, the Aldens stared at him.

"People come to a new place for a reason," Chad said. "They're looking for something — to learn or to have fun or to find . . . something. When I go to a new place, I try to find an object or a person that would make a good painting. Whenever my father goes someplace, he looks for something about his hobby."

Again Jessie wondered what Mr. Piper's hobby might be, but suddenly Benny exclaimed, "Look at the bridge!"

Ahead, traffic was stopped. The Michigan Avenue Bridge was angling up into the air.

"How will we get around it?" Henry asked.

"We'll just wait," Chad said. "It'll go down soon."

He led them to the side of the bridge. Below them, boats with tall masts moved along.

Jessie saw something else. "What's down there?"

"Lots," Chad said. "You're looking at a

tour boat landing. But there's a lower level, under the main streets."

"You mean with roads and everything?" Benny asked.

Chad nodded. "In some places there are train tracks and stores and restaurants."

"Like a double-decker city," Henry said.

The bridge moved back into place. The gates lifted. Traffic once again streamed over the bridge.

Before long, they came to the bronze lions. Violet was the first up the long stairway and through the revolving doors. The others were close behind her.

Behind the polished wood information center, a marble stairway went up to the sunlit floor above.

"This place is big," Benny said. "Where do we go first?" He was wondering where they might find tiny rooms.

Chad led them downstairs. "I thought you might like to start on the lower level," he said. "We'll pick up a brochure. But I'll have to meet you later. I have work to do."

They agreed to meet later in the lobby.

"Or, if I finish quickly, I'll look for you," Chad said as he hurried off.

Henry studied the brochure. The Aldens wandered around the museum, stopping along the way to admire displays of armor, an Egyptian mummy case, and ancient jewelry. But there were no tiny rooms.

"Where are the tiny rooms?" Jessie asked.

"We're in the wrong place," Benny said. "We have to go to the zoo."

It was nearly time to meet Chad. The Aldens headed toward the lobby.

Henry hung back. He looked at the map again. "Wait a minute!" he said.

At the same moment, Jessie stopped short. "Look!" She pointed to a sign over a doorway.

Together, she and Henry said, "The Thorne Miniature Rooms."

Inside this gallery they found tiny room after tiny room. Each represented a different time and a different place. Each held furniture and articles of the period.

The children were fascinated. They lingered at one room after another.

Finally Violet said, "Two lions and tiny rooms! We've found it!"

"But the clue says 'tiny rooms/ On the ground,'" Jessie reminded them. "These rooms aren't on the ground."

"The cases they're in are on the floor," Benny said. "Maybe the clue writer meant to say *floor*."

Violet agreed. "*Floor* didn't rhyme, so he used *ground*."

Henry was deep in thought. Finally he said, "He meant *ground*, all right. This is the ground floor."

"We've found it!" they all said at once.

"So these are the tiny rooms you were asking about," Chad said as he came up beside them. "How did you know about them?" Before they could say a word, he answered his own question. "You read about them in the brochure."

"Right," Henry said, "we read about them." He didn't go on to say, *in the second clue*.

"I'm hungry," Benny said.

Chad laughed. "Me, too. This place always makes me hungry. Probably because there are so many beautiful paintings of food."

He took them to an outdoor courtyard. They found a table near the center fountain.

They were no sooner seated than Chad said, "Oh, I forgot. I was supposed to leave a message for a friend of mine." He took a square white envelope from his back pocket. "I told him it'd be on the student bulletin board." He stood up. "I'll be right back."

As he hurried away, Jessie said, "Do you suppose that's the next clue?"

"In Chad's envelope?" Violet asked.

Jessie nodded.

"Why would he tell us that story about leaving a note for his friend?" Henry said. "He could have just given us the envelope and said he found it somewhere."

"Maybe he knows we suspect him," Benny said. "He's trying to throw us off his trail."

Jessie spotted a man across the room. Although his back was to them, he looked familiar. His dark hair circled a bald spot.

Below his suit coat, he wore overalls. "There's that man again."

They all looked at him.

Remembering the man's mustache had been crooked when they saw him at the ball game, Benny giggled.

Just then the man turned around. He had *no* mustache! And very bushy eyebrows!

"No mustache," Violet observed. "He's not the same man."

"He could have shaved it," Henry suggested.

"And put it over his eyes," Benny joked.

The man turned on his heel and hurried away.

"He certainly looks like that other man," Jessie said. "Maybe they're brothers."

They talked about that possibility until Chad returned.

He looked strange — pale and dazed. "You're not going to believe this," he said. "I think someone's following us." He held up a white envelope. "I found this on the student bulletin board. It's addressed to you!"

CHAPTER 6

Picture, Picture

After a moment's stunned silence, Henry reached out for the envelope.

Chad handed it over. "Who would leave a message for you here?"

"That's what we'd like to know," Benny said.

Even though she knew this must be the third clue, Jessie said, "Maybe it's from Grandfather." She watched Chad closely.

Henry went along with the pretense. "That could be." He, too, watched Chad closely. The young man seemed genuinely surprised to find the note here. Was he faking? There was no way to tell. "Maybe Grandfather wants us to meet him later."

"But Grandfather didn't know we would be here," Benny said.

Chad sank into a chair. "He might know," he said. "I called my father's office when we got here."

"Did you talk to Grandfather?" Henry asked.

Chad shook his head. "He and my father had gone. I left a message."

Henry folded the envelope and put it in his pocket.

Chad frowned. "Aren't you going to open it?"

"We'll read it later," Henry said.

Benny was curious about the note. "But Henry," he protested, "if it's from Grandfather —"

Just then a waiter came to take their order.

After lunch, Chad said, "I thought we might go down to the lake. Violet and I could get in some sketching."

Violet's shoulders drooped. "Oh, I didn't bring my sketchbook," she said sadly.

Chad tapped his knapsack. "I have an extra."

He led them out of the building and around the corner. At the lake, boats bobbed beside narrow piers. Out beyond the harbor, sails moved along the horizon.

"This looks like a good place," Chad said. "Does anyone else want to give it a try? I have plenty of sketch paper."

"Jessie and I will take a walk," Henry said.

Benny sighed. "I'd like to do that, too."

Chad laughed. "I'll get Violet set up." He gave her a sketchbook and several pencils.

Violet studied the scene. "I'll never get the shadows right," she said.

"You will," Chad assured her. "I'll show you how."

Henry, Jessie, and Benny walked along the lake, checking every now and then to be sure Chad wasn't watching them.

Finally Henry opened the envelope.

"Is that the same envelope Chad had?" Benny asked. "The one he was going to put on the bulletin board for his friend?"

Henry shook his head. "That one was square. This one is a rectangle." Henry carefully unfolded it. "It says 'CLUE #3.' "

Benny hopped up and down impatiently. "Read the rhyme!"

This time it wasn't a rhyme. It was a picture made up of cut-out sections from other pictures.

"A collage," Jessie said.

It showed a cow, a lantern, and burned-out buildings. In the foreground was a picture of a modern fire engine.

"Oh, this one's easy." Benny pointed at the picture. "That's Mrs. O'Leary's cow and this is her lantern — the one the cow kicked over —"

"*Supposedly* kicked over," Jessie corrected him. "Remember, Benny, that's just one possible story."

Benny waved that away. "And all these buildings — that's how the city looked after the Great Chicago Fire."

Jessie studied the picture. "I think you're right, Benny."

"But what about the fire engine?" Henry said.

"That's supposed to be one of the trucks that tried to put the fire out."

"I don't think so, Benny," Henry said. "This is a modern fire engine."

"But why would he put a picture of a new fire truck with all that old stuff?" Benny asked.

Although it looked easy, this clue could prove to be the most difficult of all.

They headed back to join Violet and Chad. On the way, they saw Willard sitting on the cement wall. His shirtsleeves were rolled up and his eyes were closed. His jacket and hat lay beside him.

"What's he doing here?" Jessie whispered.

"Following us," Benny answered.

Henry approached the man. "Let's ask him."

Jessie hung back. "Maybe we shouldn't disturb him."

But Willard's eyes snapped open and he looked right at them. He smiled. "Well,

well," he said. "If it isn't the Aldens. Still looking? Or have you found it?"

Benny glanced at his sister and brother. His look said, *I told you so.* He had been right: Willard had something to do with the treasure hunt.

"Have we found what?" Henry asked.

Willard lifted his hands, palms up. "Whatever it is you're looking for."

Benny started to say, *I think you know what we're looking for.* Before he could get it out, Jessie interrupted.

"Do you come down to the lake often?" she asked.

"Every chance I get. Especially in weather like this."

Violet called to them.

"See you later, Willard," Henry said, and the three Aldens went off.

"He's the one," Benny said.

Jessie and Henry said nothing. Each was wondering if Benny could be right after all.

Violet came running toward them. "Look at this! Chad taught me how to hold my pencil to do the shading." She showed them a sketch of a boat moored to a pier.

"This is really good," Henry said.

Chad smiled. "Violet's very talented."

Violet blushed. She did not think she was an artist yet, but there was no doubt that she was on her way to becoming one.

They strolled back to the apartment. Willard was not there. Another doorman greeted them.

Upstairs, Henry couldn't find the key. "I forgot to take it with us this morning," he explained.

"Knock on the door, Henry," Jessie suggested. "Maybe Grandfather's inside."

No one answered.

"No problem," Chad told them. "I have a key." He dug a ring of keys out of his pocket, selected one, and opened the door. Then he looked at his watch.

"You don't have to stay," Henry told him.

"I do have some work to do," he said.

"Grandfather should be along soon," Jessie said.

Knowing they would be all right without him, Chad left.

Henry took the new clue out of his pocket. "Violet, take a look at this," he said.

As Violet studied the picture, Benny explained it.

"I don't think the new fire engine is a mistake," she said.

"Neither do Henry and I," Jessie said.

"But what can it mean?" Violet asked.

Before they had time to figure it out, Grandfather came in. "Is everybody ready for dinner?" he asked.

Henry slipped the clue in with the maps and leaflets.

"Is it dinnertime already?" Benny was surprised. He had been so engrossed in the clue that he had forgotten all about eating.

Mr. Alden laughed. "Don't tell me you're not hungry, Benny!"

"Oh, I am," Benny answered. "I just didn't know it."

Willard was back on duty, and he hailed a cab.

"Where're we going?" Violet asked as she slipped into the backseat.

"To a very special place," Mr. Alden said.

The cab stopped before a brick building with striped awnings. People sat at white tables in the small front yard.

"Let's eat inside," Grandfather said.

They found a table by a bay window.

Henry went over to a display case full of photographs and other souvenirs. "This is the birthplace of deep-dish pizza," he told them when he returned.

They ordered a large pizza with everything.

"*Numero uno,*" the waiter said. "A good choice. Number one."

It was, indeed, a good choice. They had never eaten a better pizza.

On the way out, Benny said, "They deserve all those plates."

They arrived back at the apartment tired and happy.

"I think I'll go to bed," Jessie said.

They all decided to do the same.

It wasn't long before they fell asleep.

Later, the telephone woke everyone except Benny.

Grandfather answered it. His voice was muffled. Still, they heard a part of the conversation.

"No, no," he kept saying. Other words and phrases drifted in to them less clearly. "Trouble?" he said, and, "I don't want that. You'll just have to wait."

"Violet?" Jessie whispered. "Did you hear that?"

But Violet had drifted back to sleep.

In the other room, Henry lay in the dark wondering what this was about. Grandfather sounded so . . . different. Was something wrong? Could he be in some kind of trouble?

CHAPTER 7

Old Stories and New Fire Engines

"Grandfather," Henry called softly. He tapped on Mr. Alden's bedroom door.

From the kitchen, Jessie said, "Tell him breakfast is ready."

Henry called again. He waited. No sound. He opened the door and took a few steps into the room. "Grandfather's not here," Henry told the others.

"He's probably downstairs getting the paper," Benny said.

Jessie sank to a chair. "I don't think so," she said. "He had a strange telephone call last night."

"I heard that call, too," Henry said.

Benny shot to his feet. "Let's go find him!" He started for the door.

"Benny, wait!" Jessie commanded. "The phone call might have been from Mr. Piper. Grandfather was probably talking to him about the paper business."

Benny wasn't convinced. "I still think we should look —"

A key turned in the lock. The door opened. Grandfather came in, carrying a newspaper.

Smiling broadly, he said, "It's a fine morning!"

Benny rushed at him, arms outstretched. Laughing, Grandfather returned the hug.

"What's this?" he asked.

"Oh, Grandfather, we missed you!" Benny answered.

His eyes twinkled. "Perhaps I should go out more often," he said.

"We didn't know where you were,"

Henry said. He tried to keep the concern from his voice, but it seeped through.

Grandfather grew serious. "I'm sorry if I worried you. I decided to take a walk this morning."

Jessie looked at Henry. *Did the telephone call cause Grandfather to go out early this morning?* she wondered. The look in Henry's eye told her he was asking himself the same question.

Benny put his hands on his hips. "You should have told us, Grandfather," he said.

Mr. Alden smiled and took Benny in his arms.

Jessie said, "Let's have breakfast."

Benny ran over to the table. "I forgot all about eating."

"We can't let that happen," Grandfather teased.

Each poured cereal from the boxes Jessie had put on the table. They topped their choices with sliced bananas and strawberries.

"I have good news," Grandfather said. "I can be your guide today. Is there anything special you'd like to see?"

They named some of the places they wanted to see. The Museum of Science and Industry was the first on everybody's list.

"There's a real submarine there," Benny said. "And a great big model train."

Grandfather nodded. "There's so much to see and do, we could spend an entire day there."

Violet held up a leaflet. "I'd like to see the Shedd Aquarium," she said.

Henry was interested in the Field Museum of Natural History. "I'd like to see the dinosaur skeletons," he said.

"Me, too," Benny agreed.

"We'll be here a few more days," Grandfather said. "We can probably see it all." He thumbed through the pile of Chicago information.

Clue #3 was among those papers. Grandfather would surely find it. The Aldens held their breaths, wondering how they would explain it without telling him about the mystery.

Mr. Alden put the folded clue aside without looking at it. The children relaxed.

"You decide. I'm going to take a shower and change my clothes."

Henry and Benny cleared away the rest of the breakfast things and did the dishes.

Jessie unfolded the latest clue. She studied the cow and the lantern and the burned city. It all fit together except for the modern fire engine. What did it mean? "Unless we visit the place where the fire started," she said, "we'll never solve this clue."

Violet opened Grandfather's workbook to reread the section on the fire. "Cow or not, the fire started somewhere in or near Mrs. O'Leary's barn."

Henry came in from the kitchen. "Then we have to find her barn."

At his heels, Benny said, "Didn't it burn up?"

"The barn's gone," Henry said, "but there might be something on the spot where it stood — a plaque or museum or something. Seeing it might help us figure out this clue."

Jessie looked at a map. "The barn was on De Koven Street." She ran her finger along the map. "Here it is." She showed the others.

Henry put the clue in his back pocket. "That's it, then, we have to go to De Koven Street."

"Good choice," Grandfather said as he came into the living room.

"Is there a museum or something there, Grandfather?" Violet asked.

Grandfather shrugged. "Truth is, I've never been there. Never had the time. But I've always thought it would be interesting to see where the fire started."

Benny grabbed his Cubs cap and off they went.

Willard was outside. "Your car awaits." He pointed to a car at the curb and handed Mr. Alden the keys.

The children were puzzled. How did Willard know they would need a car?

Grandfather seemed to know what they were thinking. As he pulled into traffic, he said, "We could have taken public transportation, but Cob thought we might like to drive today."

Henry studied a map. "Do you know how to find De Koven Street, Grandfather? It's only a block long."

Mr. Alden nodded. "Cob gave me directions," he said.

Henry, Jessie, and Violet thought nothing of that remark until Benny asked, "How did Mr. Piper know where we were going?" It was a good question. How could Mr. Piper know where they were going when they had just decided this morning? They waited expectantly for the answer.

It never came.

Instead, Grandfather directed their attention to the sights along the way. Before long, he pulled up to a glazed red brick building. High on one corner, white letters spelled out CHICAGO FIRE ACADEMY. Near the entrance was a giant gold sculpture of flames.

"Is this a school for firemen?" Benny asked.

Violet asked, "Is this where the Great Chicago Fire started?"

"Let's go inside and see," Grandfather answered.

An old red hose wagon was displayed in the lobby. Firefighters in small groups at the information desk and in the hall beyond smiled at them as they entered. One of them stepped forward. "Welcome," he said. "Can I help you?"

They asked him about Mrs. O'Leary.

He led them to a plaque on the wall. A chain connected to two brass fire nozzles set it apart from other displays.

Henry read the inscription. "On this site stood the home and barn of Mrs. O'Leary, where the Chicago fire of 1871 started. Although there are many versions of the story of its origin, the real cause of the fire has never been determined."

"The barn was right here," the firefighter said. "The gold flame outside stands where her house was."

Jessie was impressed. "And now, on the same spot, people are trained to fight fires."

They wandered down the hall looking at the glass-covered wall displays of historical photos and drawings.

Outside, Benny's eyes grew wide. Shiny

fire trucks of all kinds filled the yard. One of the firemen helped Benny and Violet climb inside.

Henry pulled Jessie aside. "This is the place," he said. He dug the clue out of his pocket. They both looked at it. There could be no doubt. Here, just as in the picture, the past and the present stood side by side.

"Do you suppose the next clue is here?" Jessie asked.

"Keep your eyes open," Henry answered.

Benny skipped over to them. "Did you see me in that fire engine?" he asked excitedly. "I'm going to be a firefighter when I grow up!"

There was so much to see and do, they spent another hour touring the site. But they did not find the next clue.

Back at the car, Grandfather said, "It's early yet. How about visiting one of those places we talked about this morning?"

The Alden children all spoke at once, each naming a favored place.

Grandfather laughed. "I'll choose." He

opened the car door and everyone got in.

They cruised along the lake past a busy harbor and through a beautiful green park.

"Who has a map?" Benny asked.

Jessie pulled one out of her backpack.

"Why do you want a map, Benny?" Henry wanted to know.

"To see where we're going," Benny said. After a long silence, he said, "I figured it out!" Before he could say another word, Mr. Alden pulled into a big parking lot. "There it is!" Benny pointed straight ahead. "The Museum of Science and Industry!"

They scooted out of the car and hurried across the parking lot. They dashed up the broad cement stairway, past huge round columns, through tall doors, into the vast building.

They had so much fun they forgot about the mystery.

But not for long!

CHAPTER 8

The Final Clue

Grandfather pulled up in front of their apartment building. Willard was outside, talking to a man in a long raincoat and a broad-brimmed hat. Something striped was sticking out of his coat pocket.

Willard waved and came to the curb. The other man hurried inside.

Henry was the only one who noticed.

Willard opened the car doors. "Welcome back," he said.

"Does that man live here?" Henry asked.

Willard looked around. "What man?"

"The man you were talking to."

Willard laughed. "I talk to everybody!"

Grandfather came around from the driver's side. "Will you see that this car gets back where it belongs?"

Willard took the keys Mr. Alden held out to him. "Be happy to oblige," he said.

They met Chad inside. "I was looking for you," he told them. "I wanted to talk to you about tomorrow — where you want to go."

"We can talk about it now," Jessie said.

Chad shook his head. "Sorry. I can't. I have an appointment." He stepped back toward the doors. "You talk it over. I'll see you in the morning."

They headed toward the elevators.

Grandfather stopped suddenly. "Why don't you go on upstairs," he said. "I want to get a newspaper."

"Do you have the key, Henry?" Violet asked.

Henry patted his shirt pocket. "I remembered it today."

"Go along, then," Grandfather said. "I'll be up shortly."

While they were waiting for the elevator, Benny said, "It sure seems like Grandfather is reading a lot of newspapers."

"You're right, Benny," said Jessie. "He just bought one this morning."

On the way up to the twentieth floor, they talked about the museum.

"Of all the things we saw, I liked the model train best," Benny said. "It reminded me of our boxcar."

The elevator doors snapped open.

As they approached 2004, Jessie saw something. One by one, the other Aldens saw it, too. Someone had put an envelope under their door. Part of it stuck out into the hall.

Jessie picked it up. "This must be the fourth clue," she said.

Benny sighed. "We haven't even solved the third one!"

"Yes, we have, Benny," Violet said. "It was the Fire Academy." She looked at Henry and Jessie. "Right?"

Henry nodded. "Had to be," he said. He opened the door and they all went inside.

Jessie slipped off her backpack and set it on a chair. Then, she examined the envelope.

"Open it, Jessie," Violet urged.

Jessie opened the envelope. "It's another collage," she said.

Benny stood up and leaned across the table. "Of what?"

Jessie laid the paper on the table where they could all see.

"It's more like a map," Henry said.

Violet turned the paper toward her. "It's a map *and* a collage!"

She was right. The crudely drawn map was topped with cut-out pictures of all the places they had been. The Water Tower was at the top and the Museum of Science and Industry was at the bottom. In between were the Michigan Avenue Bridge, the Art Institute, Grant Park, the Fire Academy — even their apartment building and the pizza place!

"How can this be a clue?" Henry wondered aloud. He held the map up.

"There's writing on the back, Henry," Benny told him.

Henry turned the paper over. "Here we go," he said. "This says, 'The Final Clue.' " He continued reading:

> *Buried deep*
> *Beneath the rest*
> *Is the treasure*
> *I think best.*
> *Can you find*
> *A place like home*
> *Resting on*
> *A bed of stone?*

Henry stopped reading. No one said a word. He reread the clue to himself. Once, twice, three times. Finally he looked up. "Any ideas?" he asked the others.

They stared at him with wide eyes. No one knew what the clue meant.

"Who is doing this?" Jessie's tone was full of frustration.

"Chad was here when we got back," Violet reminded them. "He could have slipped the clue under the door."

"But he has a key," Henry said.

"I think Willard did it," Benny piped up.

"Willard could have brought the envelope up here," Henry said.

"And he could have made the map and written the clue, too."

"Let's go back over what we know." Jessie took the first two clues out of her backpack.

Henry removed the third clue from his back pocket and set it and the final clue beside the others. "Go back to the first day," he said.

"Willard gave us the clue about the Water Tower," Benny said.

Violet nodded. "We were waiting for Chad in the lobby."

"And Chad talked to Willard outside," Jessie added. "Then Willard gave us the envelope."

"Don't forget that other man," Henry said. "He was talking to Willard, too."

The others hadn't thought about the strange man. No one had ever suggested he had anything to do with this mystery.

Thinking about the man always made Benny giggle. "The man with the big mustache," he said. "How did it get so crooked?"

"It wasn't crooked the first time we saw him," Jessie said.

"That was later, Benny — at the ball game," Violet reminded him. "Maybe he made a mistake trying to trim it."

"Did anyone notice that man with Willard today?" Henry asked.

"The man in the raincoat?" Jessie said.

Henry nodded. "Did anyone see his face?"

No one had.

"I thought he might be the man with the mustache," Henry continued. "When we pulled up, he hurried away. It was as if he didn't want us to see him."

None of the others had noticed that.

"He had something sticking out of his pocket," Henry said. "It looked like a striped cap."

"The man at the ballpark wore a striped cap," Violet remembered.

"And the man we saw talking to Willard that morning was carrying one," Jessie added.

"Like a railroad engineer's hat," Violet said.

"So the man downstairs today could be the same man," Henry concluded.

"Let's say he gave Willard the first clue." Jessie held up the second clue. "But what about this one? I found it in my backpack after we had been to the Water Tower. We didn't see him there."

Benny frowned in thought. "Maybe he put the clue there before we got there. Or Willard — he went there early in the morning and hid the envelope."

"I looked all around that building," Henry said. "Inside and out."

"Then I dropped the leaflets," Jessie said. "We already decided I must have picked up the clue then."

"I picked up most of the leaflets," Benny said. "And I didn't see an envelope."

"And Grandfather picked up the others," Violet said. "The envelope must have been with those."

"The person who dropped that envelope knew we'd find it," Henry said. "Whoever did it had to be right there with us."

Henry smiled triumphantly. "There were only two people who could have done that: Chad or Grandfather."

Benny stood up. "Chad did it," he said. "Now can we eat?"

"Not until Grandfather comes back," Jessie said.

Suddenly they realized that Mr. Alden had been downstairs a long time — much longer than it would take to buy a newspaper.

"He always takes a long time," Benny said. "He's probably talking to Willard."

But the others weren't so sure. They remembered last night's telephone call, and Grandfather's long walk that morning. None of the Aldens could remember seeing Grandfather reading the first newspaper he'd bought.

"Let's go look for him!" Henry said.

Before he could finish the thought, Jessie was out the door, Violet at her heels.

Henry sprinted after them, saying, "Come on, Benny!"

CHAPTER 9

Another Phone Call

The elevator seemed to take forever. None of the Aldens spoke. They were wondering what they would find when they reached the ground floor. Grandfather had been strange during this trip. How did he know they would be at the Water Tower that day? He said Chad told him. No one remembered that — not even Chad. And later, at the ball game, he disappeared. He told them he stopped to buy Benny a cap, but that wasn't true. Henry was with him when he bought it. Then there was the phone call in the night. And all the trips to get newspapers! Added together, these events got the Alden children thinking.

"Maybe he decided to read the paper down in the lobby," Jessie suggested.

That was a possibility. Comfortable chairs and couches lined the inner lobby. He could read the paper *and* chat with Willard.

The doors slid open. The children hurried out. They glanced around. No one was sitting on the chairs or couches.

The Aldens looked beyond to the outer lobby. Then they saw Grandfather. Off in a corner, he was talking to someone — a man who carried a raincoat and a broad-brimmed hat.

"There he is!" Benny said, darting ahead.

Henry caught him. "Wait, Benny," he said. "Let's see what we can find out." He put a finger to his lips, a signal for his sisters and brother to be quiet.

They crept to the wall between the two rooms and pressed themselves against it. One of the doors was propped open. Still, it was difficult to hear Grandfather's words over the voices of the other people in the outer lobby. They did hear the tone; it sounded as if the two men were having a disagreement.

Henry motioned for the others to follow. He went through the doors. Then he stopped short. "Why, Grandfather!" he said, pretending to be surprised. "We were just looking for you."

Mr. Alden's face turned red and his eyes opened wide. He was genuinely surprised. He opened his mouth to speak, but nothing came out.

The other man stepped forward. He held out his hand. "I'm Jacob Piper," he said. "You must be the very special grandchildren I've heard so much about."

The children shook his hand. They all said, "It's nice to meet you."

Something about the man seemed familiar.

Henry glanced at the raincoat and hat Mr. Piper carried. "Didn't we see you here earlier?" he asked. "Talking to Willard?"

Mr. Piper looked at Mr. Alden, then back

at the children. He didn't respond. Instead, he said, "I want to take you out to dinner. I've been trying to persuade your grandfather."

Mr. Alden recovered his voice. "I told Cob you were probably too tired. After all, you've had a busy day."

Relief flooded the younger Aldens. So that's what the two men had been talking about.

"I'm never too tired to eat," Benny piped up.

Everyone laughed.

"So you'll come?" Mr. Piper said. He sounded pleased.

"We'll have to clean up and change," Mr. Alden said.

Mr. Piper turned to Benny. "Can you wait that long?"

"I think so." Benny sounded very serious — and uncertain.

Mr. Piper laughed. "Good," he said. "Meet you in an hour." He put on his hat and turned to leave. "Remember: X marks the spot," he said as he went out the door.

That seemed a strange thing to say.

"X marks what spot?" Benny asked.

"We'll find out," Mr. Alden said. "Cob is fond of riddles."

The younger Aldens were ready before their grandfather.

In the living room, Henry said, "Mr. Piper is the man we saw earlier — the man in the raincoat."

Jessie nodded. "I thought so, too, Henry. But when you asked him, he didn't answer."

"Didn't you say there was something striped sticking out of his pocket, Henry?" Violet asked.

"Yes. A railroad cap — the kind the man with the mustache wore."

"I didn't see anything like that," Benny said.

"Mr. Piper was carrying the raincoat," Henry responded. "It was all folded over. You couldn't see his pockets." He sighed. "But I was on the wrong track. He's not the man with the mustache."

Jessie sat down at the table. "Let's look over the clues again," she said.

They listed what they knew. The first clue had been given to them by Willard. The second was picked up outside the Water Tower. The third was at the Art Institute on the student bulletin board. Chad gave them that one. The fourth and final clue had been slipped under their door. Knowing where they had gotten the clues did not tell them who had written them.

"We know one thing for sure," Henry concluded. "Chad was with us — or nearby — every time."

It did seem likely that Chad was behind the mystery. But even though they had watched him for telltale signs of guilt, there had been none. He had certainly acted surprised to find the envelope on the student bulletin board. He had even suggested someone might be following them.

That thought prompted Violet to say, "Remember that man at the Art Institute? We thought he might be the man with the mustache."

"But he wasn't," Benny said. "He didn't have a mustache. Just bushy eyebrows."

"The two men did look alike," Henry said. "Both were balding and both were about the same size."

Jessie nodded. "We thought they might be brothers."

Grandfather came into the room. "Are we ready?" he asked.

Benny's stomach growled. Everyone heard it.

Mr. Alden laughed. "I think that's a *yes!*"

Because it was a warm, clear evening, they decided to walk.

Thinking about the mystery, Henry asked, "Grandfather, have you known Mr. Piper for a long time?"

"For many years. I knew his father, too. And I watched Chad grow up."

"Has he always been in the paper business?" Jessie asked.

Grandfather nodded. "And his father before him. Somewhere along the line, the family was connected with railroading. At one time, Chicago was the railroad center of the country."

That pleased Benny. "Maybe I could ask

Mr. Piper how I can get to be a railroad engineer."

Mr. Alden chuckled. "I'm sure he could help," he said. Grandfather stopped before a glass and steel building. "We're here."

The Alden children stepped back to look up. They couldn't believe their eyes. Starting at the broad base and climbing to the narrower top were a series of gigantic steel X's.

"X marks the spot," the younger Aldens all said at once.

Grandfather laughed. "Right you are," he said. "Another mystery solved!" He told them the name of the building: the John Hancock. "The X's are not decoration; they're essential to the structure," he added as he glanced upward. "This was the tallest building in Chicago until the Sears Tower was built."

They hurried inside to an elevator. It ascended so quickly their ears popped. The first stop was a restaurant on the ninety-fifth floor, where Jacob Piper was waiting.

He led them to a table by the windows.

Behind him, Henry and Jessie noticed something they hadn't seen before: Mr. Piper's dark hair framed a bald spot.

"Here we are," Mr. Piper said.

Outside the windows, the lake and city stretched as far as the eye could see.

Beside them, Mr. Piper murmured, "No matter how many times I see this sight, it still thrills me."

"And no wonder," Grandfather said. "It's spectacular."

They sat down and opened their menus.

Benny read the selections. Everything looked good. He glanced at the prices. Everything was very expensive. He closed his menu. "Maybe I'm not so hungry after all."

Mr. Piper seemed to read his mind. "This is my treat," he said. "I come here on special occasions only. Meeting you finally, and our being together — that's reason to celebrate."

After that, they all relaxed.

Mr. Piper was easy to talk to. He told them about the paper business and about his family. "I hoped Chad could join us tonight," he said, "but with work and school, he hasn't much spare time."

"Chad's a very good artist," Violet said. "And a very good teacher."

Mr. Piper smiled. "He told me you were good, too, Violet."

When their dinners arrived, Jessie said, "This looks beautiful — almost too good to eat."

Benny picked up his fork. "No food looks *that* good," he said.

Throughout the meal, Henry was distracted. Mr. Piper's upper lip and lower forehead were red, and he kept scratching them.

Benny noticed it, too, and while they were waiting for dessert, he asked, "What's that red stuff on your face, Mr. Piper?"

"Benny!" Jessie scolded.

"That's all right, Jessie," Mr. Piper said. "It does look strange. People have been asking me about it all week. It's some kind of rash."

"You must be allergic to something, Cob," Mr. Alden said.

Mr. Piper smiled. "I wonder what it could be."

Back at the apartment, the children went straight to bed. Grandfather sat down to read his newspaper.

The phone rang.

This time, all four Aldens heard it. Behind their doors, they listened carefully.

"I told you that before," Grandfather said. "You just have to be patient." And, "No, I won't do that. Not yet." There was a pause, then, "Trust me. It won't be long."

"Let's go talk to the girls," Benny whispered.

Henry shook his head. "Not now, Benny. Grandfather will hear us."

Across the hall, Violet and Jessie had a similar conversation.

For now, there was nothing they could do.

X Marks the Spot

Grandfather knocked on their doors. "Wake up, sleepyheads!" he called. "It's another beautiful day in Chicago!"

For a few brief seconds, the younger Aldens forgot their concern. But when they were fully awake, the memory of last night's telephone call resurfaced.

"Grandfather sounds cheerful," Violet said. She was hoping they had been wrong. Perhaps the two late-night phone conversations did not mean trouble after all.

Jessie slipped into her slacks. "He does,"

she agreed. But still she was fearful. Grandfather had a way of putting a good face on things. If he *was* in some kind of trouble, he would not want to worry them.

They went out into the hall. The boys' door opened and Henry and Benny came out.

"Grandfather certainly sounds cheerful," Henry said.

"He's pretending," Benny whispered.

The table was set with juice and fresh fruit and a big platter of sweet rolls.

"Well, there you are!" Grandfather said as they sat down. "I was up early," he said. "I went to the bakery." He held up a piece of paper. "But I remembered to leave a note in case you woke up and found me gone."

Jessie and Henry looked at each other. They had left the clues spread out on this table. Their maps and leaflets were stacked at one end. Were the clues there? Had Grandfather seen them? If he had, wouldn't he ask about them? How would they answer his questions?

Grandfather saw Jessie staring at the

stack. "I piled those things together," he said.

Surely he hadn't noticed the clues.

"I'll be busy all day today. What do you and Chad have planned?"

"We haven't talked to him," Henry said.

"He was here yesterday," Benny put in, "just before we found —"

Jessie was quick to interrupt. "He was here when we got back from the museum," she said, "but he didn't have time to talk."

Grandfather nodded. "That's right."

Violet said, "I'm hoping we can do some more sketching."

"It's a fine day for it." Mr. Alden pushed his chair away from the table. "I guess I'd better get a move on." He went into his bedroom.

Violet leaned close to the others. "Should we ask him about the phone calls?"

"There's probably nothing to tell us," Henry said. "He seems fine."

Mr. Alden came in carrying a briefcase. "Can you find enough to do until Chad gets here?" he asked.

They all said, "Yes. Plenty!"

As soon as he was gone, Jessie dug through the pile of brochures. "Funny Grandfather didn't see the clues," she said as she spread them out.

Violet looked at them and sighed. "Where do we start?"

"Let's not think about the writer of the clues," Henry said.

Benny tapped the final clue. "We should solve this."

Jessie turned the map over. She read the first four lines of the verse. " 'Buried deep/ Beneath the rest,' " she repeated.

"We might need a shovel for this one," Henry joked.

"Read the rest, Jessie," Benny said.

" 'Can you find/ A place like home . . .' "

"What does that mean?" Violet asked.

"*Home* could be Grandfather's house," Jessie said.

"Or our boxcar," added Violet. "After all, that was our home once."

Henry said, "The last part says, 'Resting on/ A bed of stone.' "

Jessie frowned. "This is the hardest clue yet."

Henry turned the paper over. "We've been to all the places pictured on this map."

"Could that mean this clue leads to someplace we've already been?" Jessie said.

The telephone rang. Jessie answered. It was Chad.

"Something's come up," he said. "I'm sorry, but I can't get there this morning."

"Oh, that's all right, Chad."

"I may be able to get away this afternoon," Chad went on. "If not, I'll see you tonight."

"Tonight?"

"At dinner with my father."

Jessie was confused. "But we had dinner with him last night."

After a brief silence, Chad said, "I . . . uh . . . maybe I misunderstood." He told her he would phone later and hung up.

Jessie repeated his message.

They had mixed feelings about it: On the one hand, they were sorry to miss a morning of sightseeing; on the other, they were happy to have time to work on the clue.

"Chad didn't seem to know we were with his father last night," Jessie said.

Violet was puzzled. "But he must have been invited. Mr. Piper said Chad was too busy to be there."

"Maybe Chad forgot," Benny suggested.

"Or got the dates mixed up," Henry added.

They returned their attention to the clue. But it was no use. They could not solve this part of the puzzle.

Henry turned the map this way and that, moving it close to his eyes and far away. "Look here," he said at last. He pointed to several pictures: the Water Tower, the Art Institute, the Fire Academy.

A small X was penciled on each one.

"Those are the places the clues sent us to," Violet observed.

"X marks the spot," Henry said.

Benny jumped in his chair. "Mr. Piper said that!"

"Mr. Piper can't be behind this," Jessie said. "When would he have the time? He's been at all those meetings with Grandfather." She leaned toward the map. "Are there any other X's?"

They took turns looking. On the first try, no one could find a single additional mark. Second time around, Violet saw something.

"This looks like an X." She pointed it out to the others.

"You found it, Violet!" Benny said.

Henry's mouth dropped open. "And it's on the picture of the building we're in!"

They were stunned to silence. Could this mean the final clue led right here? But where could the treasure be?

"Let's go talk to Willard," Jessie suggested. "Maybe he knows something about this building that would help."

Willard smiled as the Aldens approached. "On your way out?"

"We've been wondering about this building," Jessie told him.

"Wonderful old place, isn't it?" the man said. "Solid as a rock. They don't build 'em like this anymore."

"Are there things about it people don't know?" Violet asked.

"Ahhh, this grand old place keeps its secrets." Willard's eyes twinkled.

"What secrets?" Benny asked.

"If I told you, they wouldn't be secrets, would they, now?"

"You could tell us," Benny said. "We won't tell anyone."

Willard threw his head back and laughed. "I've been sworn to secrecy. I'm sorry," he said.

Just then several people came in. Willard went to greet them.

The Aldens looked around the lobby. Was there anything here that might help in their search? Henry noticed two doors. Painted the same color as the walls, they were barely visible.

"Wait here," he whispered. Hoping Willard wouldn't notice, he slipped across the lobby. He tried one door and then the other. Both were locked.

CHAPTER 11

Buried Treasure

Disappointed, the Aldens went back upstairs.

Just inside the apartment door, Violet picked up something. "What's this?" She held it in her open hand. It was fuzzy and black.

"It looks like some strange caterpillar," Jessie said.

Benny took it between two fingers. He held it under his nose. "Do I look like the man with the mustache?"

Jessie laughed, then grew serious. "Let me

see that." She turned it over. "The back is covered with something — dried paste or glue."

All at once, the four Aldens came to the same conclusion: "It's part of a disguise!"

"The man in the overalls wore it!" Jessie said.

"That would explain why the mustache was crooked. The glue was dry, so it no longer stuck as well," Henry said.

Violet took the object from Henry. "But it isn't big enough to be a mustache. It's more like" — she put it above her eye — "an eyebrow!"

Jessie sank to a chair. "Do you suppose . . ."

"Yes! That's it!" Henry said. "The man with the mustache and the one with the bushy eyebrows — they're one person!"

"The *same* person!" Violet said.

"*What* person?" Benny asked.

"Whoever was up here while we were talking to Willard," Henry said. "Whoever dropped the eyebrow — *that* person!"

"Chad has a key," Jessie reminded them.

"We would have seen him come into the building," Violet said.

"Unless there's another way in," Henry added.

"Maybe he hid somewhere in the hall until we went out," Benny suggested.

Jessie's mind took her in another direction. "Chad was never with us when we saw that strange man," she said. "But he was always nearby."

Slowly, the others understood her meaning. Chad could be the man in the disguise!

"But he never wore overalls," Henry said.

"Maybe he carried them in his knapsack," Benny said.

"Where would he have changed into them?" Henry persisted.

They were getting nowhere. Every question about the man led to several new questions. Finally they sat down with the clues and began listing everything they knew.

Violet puzzled over the lines "Buried deep/Beneath the rest."

"The X is marked on this building. Do

you think there could be something underneath it?" she asked at last.

Henry thought about that. Then he remembered: "Chad told us Chicago has a lower level."

"With train tracks and everything," Benny added.

"Maybe it runs under this building," Jessie said.

Benny sprang out of his chair and headed for the door. "Let's go find out!"

Downstairs, Grandfather Alden huddled with someone wearing bib overalls — a man with a mustache and one bushy eyebrow! Talking intently, the two stepped out of sight. By the time the Alden children reached the outer lobby, the men were gone.

"They didn't go out the front door," Violet said. "We would've seen them."

Henry was baffled. "But they couldn't just . . . disappear!"

"Look, Henry!" Jessie pointed to the doors Henry had tried earlier. One of them was open.

"Let's ask Willard where it leads," Violet suggested.

But Willard was busy outside.

And Benny was already across the room. His brother and sisters followed. They slipped through the door and came upon a stairwell. They heard voices below, and then . . . nothing.

Taking the lead, Henry crept down the stairs. The others stayed close behind him.

At the bottom of the stairs was another door. Slowly, cautiously, Henry cracked it open and peeked into the dimness beyond.

Henry let out a soft whistle. Then he said, "Wow!"

"What is it, Henry?" Jessie murmured.

Henry opened the door. There in the murky light was a lone railroad coach!

Stunned, they moved outside to the walkway. They wondered where the car had come from and why it was there.

After a long silence, Violet said, " 'A place like home'! The clue was about our home in the boxcar!"

" 'Resting on/A bed of stone,' " Jessie quoted.

"Gravel, or stone, is used to make railroad ties stable," Henry said.

"We've solved the final clue!" Violet said.

But the mystery was yet to be fully explained. They still had no idea who was behind this strange treasure hunt — or the reason for it.

Henry motioned them to stay where they were. He sneaked up onto the observation platform and peered through a window.

"What do you see?" Violet asked.

Suddenly a voice behind her said, "I see you've found the treasure I think best."

Jessie, Violet, and Benny spun around. Their mouths dropped open in surprise. "You!"

Jacob Piper pulled off a fake mustache and one bushy eyebrow.

Just then, Grandfather appeared on the platform beside Henry. "I told you, Cob," he said. "My grandchildren are smart. I knew they'd figure out our little game."

Jacob Piper and Grandfather! Together,

they were responsible for this baffling mystery!

Mr. Piper climbed onto the platform. "Come on aboard."

Astonished, the children followed him.

Cob swept his arm in a circle. "Welcome to my home."

Benny stared at him. "You *live* here?"

Cob laughed. "It's very comfortable," he said. He proudly showed them everything: a desk that opened into a large table; chairs that turned into beds; a stainless steel kitchen, where something bubbled on the compact stove.

"That smells good," Benny said.

"Spaghetti sauce for our supper," Cob told him.

Questions swirled through the Aldens' minds, but they were too amazed to ask them. Still, the two men provided answers.

Grandfather said, "When I told Cob you like mysteries, he planned this treasure hunt."

"It was a good way for you to see my favorite city," Mr. Piper told them. "But I was afraid you wouldn't solve it. I wanted to tell

you. Your grandfather and I argued about it."

That explained the telephone calls.

"I was worried about the whole thing," Mr. Alden continued. "I didn't know how I was going to give you the clue at the Water Tower. Fortunately, Jessie, you dropped the maps. I slipped the envelope in with them."

"And I just missed seeing Chad at the Art Institute," Mr. Piper said.

Henry found his voice. "So Chad didn't know."

Mr. Piper shook his head. "I was afraid he'd give it away."

"How about Willard?" Benny asked.

"He knew something was going on, but he never figured it out." Cob held up the mustache. "I'm not very good at this disguise business."

Benny snickered. "I never saw a crooked mustache before."

"I didn't know it was crooked!" Cob laughed.

Now Henry knew what caused Cob's rash. "You're allergic to the glue."

Cob nodded. "And I couldn't make it stick. Today I lost an eyebrow."

"We found it in the apartment," Violet told him.

Cobb nodded. "I thought I might find something in the apartment to tell me how close you were to finding this car."

"Not very close," Jessie said.

"Oh, you're good detectives," Grandfather said. "You would have figured it out."

Now that all the puzzle pieces were in place, Cob gave them a new challenge. "See if you can set the table for eight." He turned to Mr. Alden. "James, you and I will cook."

Benny counted. There were six of them. "Who else is coming?"

"Chad and Willard," Cob answered. "They didn't know it, but they played important parts in our little game."

It was tight, but they all fit. During dinner, the Aldens told Chad and Willard about the mystery and how they had solved it.

"I knew you were looking for something," Willard said.

Chad just kept shaking his head. "Dad, you planned all this?"

"And more," Mr. Piper said. "I've saved the best part for last."

Benny jumped in his chair. "Tell us! Please!"

"This is my own private train car," he began. "It belonged to my grandfather. He was in the railroad business. After he retired, he brought it to his backyard."

"We have a boxcar in our backyard," Violet said.

Mr. Piper nodded. "So James told me. And just like you, I played in it every chance I got."

Benny looked around. "This is much fancier than our boxcar."

"It didn't always look like it does today," Cob said. "Time and weather had done their work. Then one day I decided to restore it."

"By yourself?" Jessie asked.

"Yes," Cob answered. "It took a long

time. After I had finished it, I thought, why not live in it? It's been here ever since. It's my hobby — the only way I relax from the paper business. I rent the track. I travel in it, too. That's my final surprise: I have a trip planned for next week."

The Alden children's minds raced ahead of him. They exchanged excited glances.

Cob laughed. "You are quick," he said. "I can tell you've guessed it. After you've seen the rest of the city, we'll hook this car to an eastbound train and take you home to Greenfield!"

The Aldens laughed with delight.

Willard laughed, too. "I'd say you Aldens found what you were looking for!"

"Much more!" Violet said.

Mr. Piper raised his glass. "A toast to buried treasure."

Henry looked around the table at his sisters and brother, Grandfather, the Pipers, and Willard. These people were his family and friends. They were the real treasures. He raised his glass. "And to those in plain sight," he said.

THE MYSTERY IN SAN FRANCISCO

created by
GERTRUDE CHANDLER WARNER

Illustrated by Charles Tang

No part of this publication may be reproduced in whole or in part, or stored in a retrieval system, or transmitted in any form or by any means, electronic, mechanical, photocopying, recording, or otherwise, without written permission of the publisher. For information regarding permission, write to Albert Whitman & Company, 6340 Oakton Street, Morton Grove, Illinois 60053-2723.

ISBN 0-8075-5434-0

Copyright © 1997 by Albert Whitman & Company. All rights reserved. Published simultaneously in Canada by General Publishing, Limited, Toronto. THE BOXCAR CHILDREN is a registered trademark of Albert Whitman & Company.

Printed in the U.S.A.

Contents

CHAPTER

PAGE

1. The Arrival — 1
2. A Crooked Street — 15
3. Sightseeing — 26
4. Something Fishy — 35
5. More Trouble — 48
6. Out to Sea — 60
7. Another Sighting — 75
8. Sounds in the Night — 87
9. The Fish That Got Away — 96
10. The Catch of the Day — 107

CHAPTER 1

The Arrival

"There he is!" said six-year-old Benny.

The airport waiting room was crowded, but the Aldens all saw the man in the baseball cap.

Henry waved to him. "That's Uncle Andy, all right."

"But where's Aunt Jane?" Jessie said.

The Aldens had come to San Francisco to visit their grandfather's sister, Jane, and her husband, Andy Bean. Chattering excitedly, the children surrounded their uncle. He laughed as he hugged them.

"Where's Aunt Jane?" ten-year-old Violet asked.

"She had some shopping to do," Uncle Andy explained. "She's going to meet us for lunch."

Benny nodded. "Good," he said. "I'm hungry."

"We ate on the plane," twelve-year-old Jessie reminded her brother.

"But Jessie, that was hours ago," said Benny.

Uncle Andy laughed. "Same old Benny," he teased. Then he said, "Let's get your luggage."

Fourteen-year-old Henry held up his duffel bag. "We carried everything on the plane with us," he said.

Benny pointed over his shoulder. "All my stuff is in my backpack."

"Well, then, let's go," Uncle Andy said.

On the way to the parking garage, he asked, "Did you have a nice trip?"

The Aldens said, "Yes!"

"I think you'll enjoy San Francisco," their uncle told them. "It's an interesting city."

He and Aunt Jane had been staying in San Francisco for the last few weeks. They would not return home until Uncle Andy had finished his business here.

"We're happy you invited us," Violet said.

Uncle Andy smiled. "We're happy to have you," he said. "I hope you've thought about what you want to do."

"We each want to do something different," Jessie said.

Henry nodded. "I'd like to see Chinatown. I've been reading about it."

"I'd like to take a boat trip," Violet told him. She had heard about sightseeing boat tours.

"The Golden Gate Bridge is my choice," Jessie put in.

"And the cable cars!" Benny said. "Don't forget the cable cars. They remind me of our boxcar."

The Alden children used to live alone in a boxcar after their parents had died. Then their grandfather found them and took them to his beautiful home in Greenfield.

Uncle Andy nodded. "You'll see all that and more." He took out his car keys. "Here we are," he said, and opened the trunk.

The Aldens piled their luggage inside. Then they all climbed into the car.

"Where are we going?" Benny asked.

Uncle Andy started the engine. "To Fisherman's Wharf," he said. "It's a good place to begin our sightseeing."

The Aldens looked at one another and smiled. With so much to do, they knew this would be a special trip.

Before long, they were in the city. The sun shone brightly on the bay. The tall buildings seemed to sparkle. Uncle Andy drove up one steep hill and down another.

"San Francisco sure is hilly," Violet observed.

"Some people call it the City of Hills," Uncle Andy said.

The car crested a hill and started down.

"They should call it roller-coaster city," Benny said. Everyone laughed.

Soon Uncle Andy pulled into a parking space.

"There's Aunt Jane!" Violet said.

Benny was the first one out of the car. "Aunt Jane!" he called, and ran toward the woman. The other Aldens hurried after him. Aunt Jane held out her arms. Benny hugged her.

"I'm so glad to see you all!" Aunt Jane said.

"We're glad to see you, too," Jessie said.

"If it's okay with everyone, I thought we'd tour the pier first," Aunt Jane said, smiling. "That way we'll work up an appetite."

They strolled along the brick sidewalk and under a sign that read PIER 39. The place was buzzing with activity. Here, an artist sketched a visitor. There, a group posed for a photo. Everywhere, people wandered along the wooden plank walkway. They went in and out of the small shops that lined both sides of the pier.

In one shop, Violet said, "We should buy

a souvenir for Soo Lee." Seven-year-old Soo Lee was the Aldens' adopted cousin.

"I'm surprised she didn't come with you," Uncle Andy said.

"She wanted to come," Jessie explained, "but she's playing her violin in a concert this week."

"She's a really good violinist," Benny put in.

"Cousin Joe has been teaching her to play," Violet said.

"And Violet's been helping her practice," Henry added.

Aunt Jane nodded. "You children certainly know how to help people," she said. "Just like your grandfather."

"We should buy something for Grandfather, too," Jessie said. She held up a T-shirt. On the front was a picture of the Golden Gate Bridge. "Do you think he'd like this?"

"You'll be here a while," Uncle Andy said. "Why don't you wait to buy your gifts. We'll be seeing so much more."

At the far end of the pier, a carousel

whirled, its music playing. There were colorful horses on two levels.

Benny was impressed. "I've never seen a merry-go-round with an upstairs and a downstairs," he said.

Aunt Jane laughed. "How about a ride?" she said.

"Will you ride with us?" Jessie asked.

"Of course we will!" Uncle Andy answered.

The Aldens walked around the carousel. Each chose a horse to ride. Aunt Jane and Uncle Andy sat in a carriage shaped like Cinderella's. The music started and off they went. Up and down. Around and around. The bright colors along the pier streaked and blurred. Above them, the sky was like a blue dome.

When the ride was over, everyone felt wobbly. "Let's sit here until we get our land legs," Uncle Andy said, pointing to a nearby bench.

Henry said, "If we're like this from a ride on the merry-go-round, I wonder how we'd be after a ride in a boat."

"You'll soon see," Uncle Andy said. "And let me tell you, the water can be pretty choppy out in the bay."

After a few minutes, Aunt Jane stood up. "Let's take a look at the water right now," she said, and led the way to the far end of the pier.

The large, open deck was filled with people. Many of them had cameras. All of them were quiet as they looked out over the water. Far to the west, tall towers rose above the water.

"Is that the Golden Gate?" Jessie asked.

"That's right," Uncle Andy said. "It's one of the longest suspension bridges in the world."

The breeze picked up. It was chilly and damp and smelled of fish. After a while, Uncle Andy said, "Why don't we go have some lunch. I know just the place." He led them along the walk behind the shops. They heard a loud barking sound.

"What's that?" Violet asked.

"Look over the rail and you'll see," Aunt Jane told them.

Below them, sea lions lounged on large, floating platforms. Their thick, dark coats were shiny with sunlight. As the children watched, a few sea lions slipped into the water. Some stood on their back flippers and barked. Others slept through the commotion.

"I wish I had some bread or something to feed them," Benny said.

Jessie pointed to a sign. "It says don't feed the sea lions."

"They can take care of themselves," Uncle Andy said.

"Judging from the size of them, they have plenty to eat," Henry observed.

They continued along the way to a broad wooden staircase and climbed to the upper deck.

"The Eagle Café," Uncle Andy said. They went inside and took a table beside a large window.

Jessie looked around at the white walls and the green tables. "This place looks old," she said.

"It's the oldest place on the pier," Uncle

Andy said. He told them the restaurant's history.

While they waited for their lunch, they watched the boats bobbing in the water below them.

"Are those fishing boats?" Benny asked.

"Most are sailboats," Aunt Jane answered. "They tie up here."

Uncle Andy pointed to several smaller boats at the end of the dock. "Those few out there are fishing boats."

Aunt Jane said, "But most of the fishing boats are down several blocks."

After they had eaten a delicious lunch of hamburgers and french fries, Uncle Andy said, "We have a friend who owns a fishing boat. His name is Charlie. Let's walk along the wharf. Maybe we'll be able to find him."

They walked west. Pigeons waddled at their feet. Gulls flew overhead, dipping and diving.

They hadn't gone far when Uncle Andy said, "Oh, there's Charlie!"

A short, stocky man stood on a pier beside a small fishing boat. On the side of the blue and white boat were the words *Charlie's Chum*.

"That must be Charlie's boat," Violet said.

"It is," Andy said.

"Chum? Doesn't that mean friend?" Benny asked. "That's a strange name for a boat."

"Charlie's boat is like a friend to him," Aunt Jane said.

"Chum also means bait," Henry said.

Benny liked double meanings. "On second thought," he said, "that's a good name for a fishing boat."

They headed down the long pier toward Charlie. Aunt Jane waved. Charlie saw them. He did not wave back. And he was frowning.

"Charlie, what are you doing here?" Uncle Andy asked as they approached. "Aren't you usually docked down the way with the rest of the fishermen?"

Charlie nodded. "Herring season," he explained. "They were overcrowded. A few of us agreed to dock here."

"Charlie, I want you to meet my brother's grandchildren," Aunt Jane said. "They've been wanting to meet a fisherman."

Charlie glanced at the Aldens. He nodded a greeting, but he did not smile. "Good you met me today," he said. "I might not be a fisherman tomorrow."

Uncle Andy cocked his head to one side. "More trouble?" he asked.

Charlie didn't seem to hear the question. He looked over his shoulder. Henry followed his gaze. Not far away, a tall man in a dark suit and sunglasses leaned against a rail, staring at them. When Charlie caught his eye, he quickly looked away.

I wonder who that man is, Henry thought. *He sure doesn't seem dressed for a day at the pier.*

"We just toured Pier Thirty-nine," Aunt Jane said to Charlie, startling Henry out of his thoughts.

Charlie turned back to the Aldens. Shaking his head, he said, "Everybody wants to visit Pier Thirty-nine."

"We liked it a lot," Benny said.

"We've never seen anything quite like it," Jessie added.

"It's nothing but window dressing for the tourists," Charlie said. "Wait till you get a taste of the real wharf."

Down the way, a young woman called, "Charlie!" Her long, red hair glistened in the sunlight.

"I think someone's calling you," Violet said.

Charlie turned. "That's Kate Kerry," he said. "She's working for me and going to school, too. Putting herself through college." Then he added, "There're some fish I have to fry," and he hurried off without saying good-bye.

Puzzled, the Aldens watched him go.

"Charlie just isn't himself these days," Uncle Andy said as he shook his head.

CHAPTER 2

A Crooked Street

Uncle Andy suggested that they continue along the wharf. "I'll show you where Charlie usually docks."

They passed big sightseeing boats. Aunt Jane stopped at the ticket booths to collect information. "So we'll be prepared for our tour," she explained.

A block away, at open-air fish markets, men prepared giant crabs for steaming kettles. Inside, people sat at tables with checkered cloths enjoying fresh fish dishes.

They came to an open section. At the

railing, Uncle Andy said, "Look down there."

The Aldens looked over the side. Below them fishing boats — small and large — rocked beside high wooden posts. No docks separated the crafts.

"How do the fishermen get on their boats?" Violet asked.

Uncle Andy pointed out the metal ladders leading down to each boat.

"I can see why Charlie had to dock somewhere else," Benny observed. "This place is filled up."

Aunt Jane headed toward the car. "Let's go home," she said. "It's time you children were settled in."

Benny skipped after her. "Is your friend Charlie a fisherman *and* a cook?" he asked.

Uncle Andy opened the car door. "A cook? Charlie? What makes you think that, Benny?"

Benny climbed into the backseat. "He said he had to fry some fish."

Uncle Andy eased into the driver's seat. "That's just an expression," he said. After everyone was inside the car, Uncle Andy started the engine and soon they were on their way.

"I've never heard that expression before," Violet said. "About frying fish. What does it mean?"

"It means he has some business to take care of," Uncle Andy explained.

"What kind of business?" Benny asked.

"Fishermen lead busy lives," Aunt Jane answered. "They're out on the water before dawn, and when they come back to shore, they have to take care of their catch."

"I don't think Charlie was talking about ordinary business, though," Uncle Andy said. "There's been trouble on the wharf."

"Trouble?" Henry repeated. "What kind of trouble?"

Uncle Andy shrugged. "Charlie hasn't wanted to talk about it, but I know something is bothering him."

"That explains it," Benny said.

In the front seat, Aunt Jane turned to look at him. "Explains what, Benny?"

"Well, he wasn't very friendly."

"Benny, that's not polite," Violet said.

"It's okay, Violet. Benny's right," Uncle Andy said.

"That wasn't like Charlie at all," Aunt Jane said. "He must be very worried about something."

They slowed down. "Look to your left," Aunt Jane told them. "We rent the second house right down there."

The sign said LOMBARD STREET. Underneath it, the narrow road zigzagged down the hill. Houses and flower gardens were perched on either side. The Aldens were amazed.

"I've never seen such a crooked street," Henry said.

"And I doubt you'll ever see another one," Uncle Andy told him. "This block of Lombard Street is said to be the crookedest street in the world."

He pulled into a garage underneath a white house. Benny hopped out. "Don't go inside yet," Benny said. "I want to see something."

The others followed him. Then they

stood watching as Benny dashed down the brick street. He didn't go far, though, and after a few seconds, he came trudging toward them.

"Eight!" he said. "There are eight sharp turns!" He stopped to catch his breath.

Uncle Andy chuckled. "Much easier going down than coming up. Right, Benny?"

Inside, Aunt Jane showed them to their rooms. The boys had one, the girls another. Each room had a view of the bay below. They unpacked and then met on the deck outside their rooms. The view was thrilling.

Henry dug a guidebook out of his back pocket. He looked at a map. "See that tower?" he said. "It's called Coit Tower. It was built to look like a fire hose nozzle. It's a tribute to the firemen who fought the earthquake fires in 1906."

Benny shivered. "I hope there's no earthquake while we're here," he said.

Jessie said, "I've been thinking about Charlie. I wonder what could be bothering him."

"Maybe he didn't catch many fish today," Benny suggested.

"Fishermen are probably used to bad days," Violet said.

"Uncle Andy mentioned trouble," Henry said. "I saw a man on the wharf. He was acting strangely. I wonder if he has anything to do with the trouble."

"The one in the suit?" Jessie asked.

"I saw that man, too," Violet said.

"He seemed out of place," Henry said. "He was so dressed up."

Benny hadn't noticed the man. "Maybe he was sightseeing like us," he suggested.

Henry shook his head. "I don't think so."

"He was staring right at us," Violet said.

"At Charlie, not us," Jessie corrected.

"And when Charlie looked at him, he turned away," Henry said.

Benny smiled. "Great! Another mystery," he said. "I'm ready!"

By the time they came downstairs, Aunt Jane was preparing supper. "I thought we'd eat here in the kitchen tonight," she said.

"It looks like home," Benny said. He was thinking of Grandfather Alden's big, airy kitchen in Greenfield, where they all lived.

Henry offered to set the table. Aunt Jane showed him where she kept the plates and silverware.

"Is there anything we can help you with?" Jessie asked.

Aunt Jane said, "No, thank you. Everything's ready. We had such a big lunch, I wasn't sure what to fix. I decided on a little of this and a little of that."

She carried a large platter of meats and cheeses to the table. To that, she added a basket of bread, a bowl of fruit, and a pitcher of cold milk.

Benny rubbed his hands together. "I'll have a little of everything," he said. They made sandwiches and ate fruit. Benny drank two glasses of milk.

When they had finished eating, Jessie asked, "Do you know that woman — the one who works for Charlie?"

"Kate Kerry," Uncle Andy said. "We've

met her. She's been working for Charlie for a while. But I can't say we really *know* her."

"Why do you ask?" said Aunt Jane.

"I just wondered," Jessie said.

"Has she heard about the trouble Charlie's having?" Henry asked.

"I can't say for certain," Uncle Andy answered. "Charlie doesn't talk about it much."

"Charlie's not one to complain," Aunt Jane said.

Henry looked at his uncle. "Is Charlie the only one having trouble?"

Uncle Andy shook his head. "I don't think so."

When they were finished eating, the children cleared the table. Uncle Andy got out the maps so they could plan their next day.

"Refresh my memory," Uncle Andy said. "What was it you wanted to see?"

The Aldens all spoke at once. Aunt Jane held up her hands. "One at a time," she said.

"I have an idea," Uncle Andy said. He opened a drawer and took out paper and pencil. "Each of you write down what you most want to see."

Uncle Andy got his baseball cap from a hook near the back door. "Now, put the papers in my hat."

Each Alden dropped a folded piece of paper into the cap. "Now what?" Benny asked.

"Nothing yet," Uncle Andy answered. "We'll just leave this here." He put the cap on the counter near the phone. "Let everything sit till morning. Then I'll pick a paper. Where we go will be a surprise."

Aunt Jane smiled at her husband. "Andy Bean, you are full of good ideas."

The Aldens weren't so sure this was a good idea. They were so excited they didn't know if they could wait until morning to find out where they would go first.

"We'd better get to bed early," Andy suggested. "We want to be rested for whatever comes."

That did seem like a good idea. The sooner they went to sleep, the sooner morning would come. Upstairs, Benny said, "I'm too excited to sleep. I'll probably lie awake all night trying to figure out which place we'll see first."

The other Aldens smiled at one another. They knew Benny would soon be sound asleep.

CHAPTER 3

Sightseeing

First thing in the morning, Aunt Jane said, "Andy, here's your cap." She handed him the baseball cap containing the four slips of paper.

"Hurry, Uncle Andy!" Benny said.

The Aldens watched as Uncle Andy reached into the hat. He drew out a piece of paper and looked at it.

"What does it say?" Violet asked.

Uncle Andy smiled. "I think I'll keep it a surprise," he said, and put the paper in his pocket.

At first the Aldens were disappointed. They didn't want to wait another minute to find out where they were going.

Then Jessie said, "That's a good idea, Uncle Andy."

Henry agreed. "The longer the wait, the better the surprise."

"Let's get going!" Benny urged. "We can wait on the way."

Violet laughed. "What about breakfast, Benny?"

"Oh," Benny said. "I forgot."

They all laughed. It wasn't like Benny to forget about a meal.

"We'll eat breakfast out," Aunt Jane said. "I know the perfect place."

And off they went.

Clang! Clang! went the cable car as it came down the hill toward them. When it stopped, Uncle Andy said, "Hop on!"

"Watch your step!" the friendly conductor called out.

Benny was the first one aboard. Riding a cable car was what he most wanted to do.

He led the way to the front section, where the sides were open and the long benches faced out.

Uncle Andy said, "So what do you think, Benny? Is this what you expected?"

"Better!" Benny answered. He had seen pictures of the cable cars. But looking at pictures was not the same as actually riding in one. It was a thrill to rumble and creak up one hill and down another.

"Benny's lucky," Violet said. "He got his wish first."

Andy said, "I didn't pick Benny's paper out of my hat. But he *is* lucky. We can take cable cars to many of the places we'll go."

Benny smiled. He was happy to know this was not his last ride.

The cable car stopped in a park. "End of the line!" the conductor called. The Aldens clambered down the steps.

When everyone had left the cable car, it moved onto a big turntable. The motor-men gripped the side rails on the wooden circle and pushed the cable car completely around. Now it was ready for its return trip.

"Wow!" Benny said. "They don't have anything like that in Greenfield!"

Aunt Jane put her arm around his shoulders. "San Francisco is a unique place, all right," she said.

"Let's eat," Uncle Andy said.

Benny smiled. "Aunt Jane's right, Uncle Andy. You are full of good ideas."

They crossed the street to the Buena Vista Café. They sat at a table beside the window and watched people line up for the cable cars. As soon as a car left, another line formed. Along the street, craftsmen sold their wares and musicians played. Beyond, the bay glimmered in the morning light.

"*Buena Vista* means 'beautiful view,' " Aunt Jane told them.

"That's a perfect name," Violet said.

The Aldens and the Beans ate hearty breakfasts of bacon, eggs, toast, and pancakes.

Afterward, they boarded a cable car heading south.

Before long, Uncle Andy said, "This is our stop." They hopped off the car and followed Andy to Grant Street. There they stopped before a tall arch with a green tile roof. Colorful dragon figures decorated the top.

"Henry, I think you'll recognize this," Aunt Jane said.

Henry nodded. "It's the Chinatown Gate."

They passed under the arch into a different world. The narrow streets were crowded with traffic. Colorful signs written in Chinese characters lined the way.

They wandered in and out of shops filled with unusual things. It was hard to resist the hand-carved animals and beautiful clothing. After they had finished shopping, the happy group went down another street into a park. They sat on a bench to rest.

Just then, Violet noticed a young woman across the street. She was coming out of a restaurant. "Isn't that Kate Kerry, the woman who works for Charlie?" she asked.

The other Aldens saw the young woman. She was wearing a yellow slicker with a hood.

"It looks like her," Jessie said, "but I can't tell. She's too far away."

Benny stood up. Waving, he jumped up and down. "Hello! Kate!" he called.

"Benny, don't do that," Jessie said, laughing.

The woman looked toward them. When she did, the hood fell to her shoulders. Her red hair glistened in the sunlight.

"It's her, all right," Benny said. He kept waving.

The woman did not return Benny's greeting. Instead, she hurried around the corner and disappeared.

"That's strange," Benny said. "She didn't even wave."

"I don't think it's strange at all," Jessie said. "She doesn't know us."

Charlie had not introduced them. Benny had forgotten that.

"But she knows *us*," Uncle Andy said.

"Oh, Andy," Aunt Jane said, "she probably didn't see us."

"Maybe it wasn't Kate," Violet suggested. "Jessie is right. She was too far away to tell for sure."

"What about the red hair?" Benny asked.

"A lot of people have hair that color," Violet said.

"Well, she sure did look like Kate," Benny said.

Aunt Jane stood up. "How about lunch? I know the perfect place. Follow me."

A few minutes later, the Aldens entered a crowded restaurant and forgot all about the young woman they had seen. They took seats and looked around.

"Where are the menus?" Jessie asked.

"There are no menus here," Aunt Jane answered.

"How do we order?" Benny asked.

A woman pushed a cart to their table. On it were many small dishes with food on them.

Cart after cart rolled up. The Aldens and

the Beans took some of the small dishes off the carts and sampled everything.

Benny sat back. "I'm full," he said. He noticed a sign. It read DIM SUM. "What does that mean?" he asked.

Uncle Andy shrugged. "Little . . . things."

"I think it means 'little delights' or 'little pleasures,' " Aunt Jane said.

"Whatever it means, it sure tastes good," Benny said.

Violet said, "I've never been to a restaurant that didn't have a menu." She was wondering how they would pay for their lunch. There were no prices listed anywhere.

Uncle Andy seemed to read her mind. "We pay according to the number of empty plates on our table," he explained.

Benny's eyes widened. He began to count the small dishes. When he reached twenty-five, he said, "Wow! This could be expensive!"

But to the Aldens' surprise, the food wasn't expensive at all.

CHAPTER 4

Something Fishy

With the afternoon still ahead of them, they returned to Fisherman's Wharf.

"Let's take a boat ride," Aunt Jane suggested.

"Oh, yes, let's!" Violet said. A boat ride was what she most wanted to do.

"But Violet, it's not your turn," Benny protested. "We didn't pick your paper out of Uncle Andy's hat."

"Your paper wasn't chosen, either," Jessie

reminded him. "But we've already been on the cable cars three times."

"Besides," Henry added, "we're at the wharf. It would make sense to take a boat ride now."

"I guess you're right, Henry," Benny agreed.

Aunt Jane smiled. "You children always work things out," she said proudly.

"There's Charlie," Uncle Andy said. "Let's ask him which boat to take. I'm sure he knows which sightseeing business has the best tours."

Charlie was on the dock beside his boat. When he saw them, he waved.

"He seems friendly today," Benny said.

"The trouble must be over," Violet decided.

Charlie met them on the walkway. "I didn't think I'd see you again so soon," he said.

"We're going to take the children on a boat trip," Aunt Jane told him.

"We thought you'd know which is the best," Uncle Andy added.

"Sightseeing tours?" Charlie said. "That's no way to see the bay. The best way to see it is on a working fishing boat."

"Like yours?" Benny asked. He couldn't imagine anything more fun than a trip on *Charlie's Chum*.

"Like mine," Charlie said. He smiled broadly. "Would you like to come fishing with Kate and me tomorrow morning?"

The Aldens didn't have to think about it. They all said, "Yes!"

"It's hard work," Charlie warned.

"We like work," Benny said.

Just then, Kate Kerry came up to them. She was wearing jeans and a white T-shirt. Her red hair was braided. "Charlie, I have to talk to you," she said. Then she smiled at Aunt Jane and Uncle Andy. "Oh, hello." She looked at the children.

"These are the Aldens," Charlie said.

"They're my brother's grandchildren," Aunt Jane said.

Kate shook hands with each of the children. "Didn't I see you here yesterday?"

"Yes," Violet answered.

"And today!" Benny said. "We saw you today, too."

Kate frowned. "Today? Where?" she asked.

Just as Benny said "Chi — " a tall, dark-haired man ran up.

"Charlie!" he said. "What're you trying to do? Ruin my business?"

Charlie looked flabbergasted. "Vito . . . I . . . I . . ."

"Fresh fish! That's what I need! Not rotten fish!"

"Rotten fish?" Charlie said. "What are you talking about, Vito?"

"Yesterday's order. Half of it was rotten. You think my customers want rotten fish?"

Charlie straightened his shoulders. He stood up tall. "My fish are always fresh," he said. "Always. In all my years, no one has ever complained about my fish."

"Well, I'm complaining," Vito shot back. "And if it ever happens again — "

"Listen here, Mr. Vito Marino, maybe it's *you*," Charlie interrupted. "Maybe you don't know a fresh fish when you smell one."

Vito's mouth dropped open. He seemed to be searching for words. Finally he turned on his heel and stalked off.

"Who was that?" Henry asked.

"Vito Marino," Charlie answered. "He owns a restaurant on the wharf. It's called Vito's Vittles."

"Vito's Vittles," Benny repeated. He thought that was a funny name. He was about to laugh when he saw Henry's warning glance.

"That's what I wanted to talk to you about," Kate said. "Vito's been telling everyone on the wharf that you sold him rotten fish."

"What? That's not true," Charlie said.

Another man joined the group. He was tall and blond. "Great day for fishing, wasn't it?" he asked. Then, noticing Charlie's worried expression, he asked, "What's the problem, Charlie?"

"Oh, Joe," Charlie said. Then he told Joe

about Vito. "Can you believe it?" he concluded. "Me, selling rotten fish?"

Joe shook his head. "Nobody needs this," he said. "If I'd been at it as long as you, Charlie, I'd be thinking of pulling in my nets." Still shaking his head, he wandered off.

"Now, who was that?" Benny asked.

"Joe Martin," Kate answered. "He's a fisherman, too."

"He looks very young," Uncle Andy observed.

"He's new to the business," Charlie said. "But he's a good man. With a little time, he'll be a good fisherman."

Jessie saw someone else — another man — down the way. Although he was dressed casually, she was sure he was the man they had seen lurking here yesterday. She was about to ask if Charlie recognized him when he disappeared behind a building.

"Charlie, perhaps we should wait a day or two before the children go out on your boat," Aunt Jane said.

Charlie looked at her. "Why should we wait?"

"Well, with this trouble and all," Aunt Jane explained. "I just thought that maybe — "

Charlie waved that away. "I'm not the first fisherman to have trouble," he said. "And I won't be the last. Besides, the routine doesn't change." He glanced at the children. "With all this sightseeing, do you think you'll be up to it?" he asked them. "We sail before dawn."

The Aldens looked at Uncle Andy. He would have to drive them to the pier.

"Is that too early, Uncle Andy?" Jessie asked.

Uncle Andy took a deep breath. "Before dawn? That *is* awfully early." He sounded serious, but there was a twinkle in his eyes.

"Oh, you're teasing," Benny said.

Before Uncle Andy had a chance to answer, Kate spoke up. "I have an idea," she said. "Why don't you children stay with me."

Aunt Jane said, "That's nice of you, Kate,

but we wouldn't want to put you to any trouble."

"It's no trouble," Kate assured her. "I'm right over there." She pointed behind her. "It'd be fun having company, and it'd save time in the morning."

Benny was staring off into the distance. "I don't see any houses," he said. "Just boats."

"I live on a boat," Kate said. "That red and white one right down there."

"It doesn't look like a houseboat," Violet said.

"It isn't," Kate said. "It's a sport fishing boat. But there're plenty of bunks. Would you like to stay with me?"

"Oh, yes!" Jessie said. She paused before adding, "If it's all right with Aunt Jane."

Kate said, "Well, Mrs. Bean, what do you say?"

Aunt Jane laughed. "I haven't much choice," she said. "Not with these children. Once they've made up their minds, there's no arguing with them. Just like their grandfather." There was pride in her voice.

"Well, that's settled," Uncle Andy said. "Let's go back home, Jane, and get these new fishermen a change of clothes."

"Give me your packages, children," Aunt Jane said. "We'll take them back home."

The Aldens handed her the things they had bought.

"Bring jackets," Charlie said. "It can get mighty cold out there some mornings."

Kate led the children to her boat. On the way, Violet asked, "Have you lived here long?"

"On and off," Kate answered. "The boat belongs to a friend of mine. He takes out fishing parties. When he's away, he lets me live on the boat."

"Charlie said you're going to college," Henry told her. "What are you studying?"

"Marine biology."

"What's that?" Benny asked.

"It's the science of living things in the sea," Kate explained. She stepped off the dock onto the deck of the boat. "Be careful," she warned the others.

One by one, they jumped onto the deck.

"Look around, make yourselves comfortable," Kate said. "I have to go back to help Charlie."

"May we help, too?" Jessie asked.

Kate shook her head. "Rest up. You'll have plenty of work to do tomorrow." She hopped back onto the dock. "Will you be all right?"

Henry nodded. "We'll be fine. Don't worry about us."

When she was out of sight, Benny said, "We forgot to ask her about Chinatown."

"That wasn't Kate we saw," Violet said.

"What makes you so sure?" Jessie asked.

"Her hair, for one thing. Kate's is braided. That woman's wasn't."

"She could have braided it after we saw her in Chinatown," Jessie said.

That was possible, Violet thought. "But what about the yellow slicker? Kate's not wearing one."

"Maybe it's here," Benny said, heading toward the cabin door.

Jessie called him back. "Don't snoop, Benny."

"Kate said to look around," Benny reminded her.

"She didn't mean we should go through her things," Jessie said.

Sighing, Benny sank into a deck chair.

"It's not important, Benny," Henry said.

"Right," Violet agreed. "And it has nothing to do with the trouble on the wharf."

"I'll bet that man has something to do with it," Jessie said.

Puzzled, the other Aldens looked at her.

"You know — the man we saw yesterday, the man in the suit. He was here again today."

Henry was surprised. "I didn't see him."

"He was in different clothes, but I'm sure it was the same man," Jessie said. "He went behind a building when Joe Martin got close to him."

"Maybe he added the rotten fish to Charlie's catch," Violet suggested.

"Somebody would have seen him do that," Henry said. "Especially yesterday. In that suit, he really stood out. We all noticed him, didn't we?"

"Not me," Benny said. "I didn't see him."

They sat quietly, thinking. The boat rocked gently. Overhead, gulls called to one another.

After a while, Benny began to giggle. "Vito's Vittles," he said. "That is the funniest name for a restaurant." No one else said anything.

Benny paused. Then he said, "What does that word mean: *vittles?*"

"Oh, Benny, you should know that word," Henry said. "It's your favorite thing."

Benny frowned. "My favorite thing?" he said. "Let me see . . ." Slowly, his face relaxed into a big smile. "Oh, I get it. Vittles means food."

Now everyone laughed.

CHAPTER 5

More Trouble

"Aunt Jane and Uncle Andy are already back with our clothes!" Violet said. "Let's go meet them."

She stepped off the boat onto the dock. The other Aldens followed her, excited that they'd be staying on Kate's boat that night.

Their aunt and uncle were visiting with Charlie on the pier near *Charlie's Chum*. Charlie was filling his fuel tank. Kate was checking the fish nets to be sure there were no big tears in them.

"Let's ask Kate about Chinatown," Benny whispered.

"Not now, Benny," Jessie said. "She's busy."

Uncle Andy waved as the children approached.

Aunt Jane held up a duffel bag. "We brought your clothes. Nice warm ones."

A man hurried toward them calling, "Charlie! Charlie!"

Charlie squinted in the man's direction. "That's Tony Gregor," he said. "Looks like more trouble."

"Someone untied my boat!" Tony said. "It floated away!" He gestured toward the bay.

"Who could have done such a thing?" Kate wondered aloud.

The children looked at each other. They thought they knew the answer: the mysterious man in the suit. But they didn't say anything. They had no proof.

"Calm down, Tony," Charlie said.

Tony walked in circles. "I don't know how much longer I can take this."

Charlie put his hand on Tony's shoulder.

Tony stopped his nervous pacing. "What am I going to do?" he asked.

"I'll take you out. We'll get your boat," Charlie said.

Tony seemed relieved. "Thanks, Charlie."

Just then, another boat pulled in beside the narrow pier.

Joe Martin tossed a line over a wooden post. "Hey, Tony, what're you doing here?" he shouted over the sound of the engine. "I just passed your boat on my way in."

That's strange, Henry thought. Earlier, Joe Martin had said he'd had a great day of fishing. Why would he have taken his boat out again? Henry decided not to ask.

Tony told Joe what had happened.

"We were just going out to get it," Charlie said.

"I'll take you, Tony," Joe said. His boat was running, ready to go.

Tony jumped aboard. Joe backed the boat away from the dock and turned it around. Hands on his hips, Charlie stood watching them. His face was creased with worry.

"Say, Charlie," Uncle Andy said, "why don't you come have supper with us. Take your mind off all this."

"Thanks," Charlie responded. "But I couldn't eat. Not now. And I have some work to do."

"How about you, Kate?" Aunt Jane asked.

"I'll stay with Charlie," she answered. She turned to the Aldens. "I'll meet you back here later, okay?"

Aunt Jane left the children's clothes with Kate. Then the Aldens and the Beans walked along the waterfront.

"Is everybody hungry?" Uncle Andy asked.

At first, no one — not even Benny! — was. They were too concerned about the trouble on the wharf to think of food.

Soon, though, the sights and smells along the wharf captured their attention.

"I changed my mind," Benny said. "I'm hungry."

It was such a lovely evening, they decided to eat outside. They bought crab and shrimp cocktails from the outdoor stands and ate them as they strolled near the water.

Far to the west, the sun dropped below the horizon.

"Oh, look!" Jessie said. She pointed toward the Golden Gate Bridge. Its supporting towers stood out against the rosy orange sky.

"What a beautiful sight!" Violet said. She wished she had brought her sketchbook.

Jessie took a deep breath and let it out slowly. "I can't wait to see the bridge up close," she said.

"Maybe we'll go tomorrow after your fishing trip," Aunt Jane told her.

Jessie smiled. That was something to look forward to.

They stopped at Pier 39 for ice-cream cones. Then they headed back toward Charlie's. Aunt Jane and Uncle Andy were in the lead; the Aldens trailed along behind them. Henry stopped suddenly.

"What's the matter, Henry?" Jessie asked.

"I think someone's watching us," he said.

Violet looked over her shoulder. She

quickly turned back. "It's that man again — the one in the suit."

Walking backward, Benny said, "I don't see anyone."

Henry whirled around.

The man was gone.

By the time the Aldens reached the dock, Tony Gregor and Joe Martin had returned.

"Now that everything's shipshape," Charlie said, "I'm going home. I could use a good night's sleep." He turned to Tony. "Do you want a ride?"

Tony shook his head. "I'm staying with my boat tonight," he said. "I don't want it to disappear again."

"That won't happen," Joe assured him. "I'll bet it was an accident. Your knot probably came loose."

Tony glared at him. "My knots never come loose," he said.

Joe shrugged. "Take it easy, Tony. I only meant . . . well, there's always a first time."

Mumbling to himself, Tony headed toward his boat, which was tied to a dock down the way.

Joe watched him. "What did I say?" he asked. Then he smiled at everyone. "Well, I'm off, too. See you in the morning." He ambled away.

Kate picked up the Aldens' duffel bag. "I suppose we should settle in, too," she said.

The Beans hugged their nieces and nephews. "We'll meet you here tomorrow," Aunt Jane told them.

"Be careful," Uncle Andy said.

"Don't worry," Kate said. "I'll keep an eye on them."

The Beans and Charlie headed for their cars.

On Kate's boat, she and the Aldens sat on the open deck. Boat lights bobbed in the dark waters. Overhead, stars shimmered.

"That was too bad about Tony's boat," Benny said. "Do you think it was an accident like Joe said?"

"I doubt it," Kate answered. "There's been too much going on. Someone untied that boat."

"But why?" Jessie asked.

"If Tony lost his boat, he couldn't fish," Violet said.

Kate nodded. "You're right."

"Why would anyone want to keep Tony from fishing?" Henry asked.

Kate shrugged.

"Don't forget the rotten fish," Jessie said. "Vito was really angry. If he quit buying Charlie's fish, what would Charlie do?"

"He'd probably have to quit fishing," Kate answered. "In the old days, there were many more fishermen. The restaurant owners bought all their fish from them. But things have changed. Much of the fish is trucked in from other places. Vito could buy fish from far away."

"It looks as if someone is trying to make all the fishermen quit fishing," Henry concluded.

They fell silent, thinking about the trouble on the wharf.

After a while, Violet yawned. "All this sea air makes me tired."

"And all your sightseeing," Kate added.

That reminded Benny about Chinatown. "Were you sightseeing, too?" he asked Kate.

Kate laughed. "Today? Me? Sightseeing? No way."

"What were you doing in Chinatown, then?"

"I wasn't in Chinatown," Kate said. Then she stood up and stretched. "I think it's about time we turned in."

The Aldens followed her inside the cabin. Bunks lined its sides. A door in the middle opened onto a staircase.

"You take the downstairs," Kate said. "I'll sleep up here."

When the Aldens were tucked into their bunks, Benny said, "She was in Chinatown, all right."

"She said she wasn't," Violet said. "I don't think she would lie."

"She didn't want to talk about it," Benny persisted. "She changed the subject right away."

Henry rolled onto his side. "I don't want to talk about it, either," he said. "I just want to go to sleep." He closed his eyes.

Jessie, Violet, and Benny followed his example.

Henry suddenly remembered something. "Joe said he passed Tony's boat on the way in," he said. "But he docked his boat right after Vito came to complain about the rotten fish. Why would he take his boat out again?"

No one answered him. They were all asleep.

Soon Henry, too, drifted off to sleep.

Later that night, something woke Jessie. She sat up, listening.

Across the room, Henry whispered, "Did you hear that?"

Jessie crept to the window.

Henry followed. "It sounded as if someone had dropped something."

"Look!" Jessie said.

Down the way, a light moved along the dock between Joe's and Charlie's boats.

"That's not a flashlight," Henry observed. "It's flickering."

The light went out.

Jessie and Henry looked at each other. Each had the same question: *Is someone tampering with one of the boats?*

Neither had an answer.

CHAPTER 6

Out to Sea

It was still dark when Kate woke them. "Dress warmly," she said.

The Aldens hurried into their jeans and sweatshirts. They tied their jackets around their waists.

Fruit, juice, and toast awaited them. Kate filled a large thermos. "Hot cocoa," she said. "It tastes really good out there in the fog." She slipped a black poncho over her head and started for the door. "I'll meet you at Charlie's."

When she had gone, Violet said, "You

see, Benny? A black poncho. Not a yellow slicker. We didn't see her yesterday in Chinatown."

"Maybe she has two raincoats," Benny said.

At the door, Henry said, "Let's go. The fish are waiting."

Outside, fog hovered over the water and clung to the docks. Far off, a foghorn blared.

When they reached *Charlie's Chum*, it seemed deserted.

"Where's Kate?" Jessie wondered aloud. "She said she'd meet us here."

Just then, Charlie appeared on deck. His gray hair was tangled and his eyes were sleepy. "Right on time," he said. He stretched and yawned. It looked as if he had just awakened.

Henry said, "I thought you went home last night."

Charlie smoothed his hair with his hands. "I couldn't sleep. Kept thinking something would happen to the boat. So I came back here."

That explained the noise Henry and Jessie had heard and the light they had seen. They were relieved to know there had been no foul play.

Kate ran up to them. "I went to buy some juice," she said and held up a brown paper bag.

When the Aldens were on the boat, Kate untied the rope and hopped aboard. After everyone had put on a life vest, Charlie backed the boat away from the dock and turned it around.

Sea lions barked at them as *Charlie's Chum* passed by on its way out into the bay. Gulls hovered overhead. One gull flew just ahead of them.

"Look!" Benny said. "That bird's leading the way!"

Far off, foghorns sounded. The air was brisk. Before long, the Aldens slipped into their warm jackets. As they neared the Golden Gate Bridge, the water became rough. The boat bumped over the surface.

CHARLIE'S CHUM

"Hang on!" Charlie shouted above the noise of the engine and the sea. The Aldens didn't need to be told.

They passed under the bridge. Jessie looked up, hoping to see the underside of the bridge, but it was too foggy to see much.

In open waters, Charlie slowed the engines. He and Kate lowered the nets into the water.

"What can we do?" Henry asked.

"That's it for now," Kate said. "Just relax and enjoy the ride."

The sun was beginning to burn through the fog. The water glimmered. The boat rose and fell.

In the distance, Henry spotted something. "Look!" he called. "A water spout!"

"Whales," Kate said.

Suddenly a whale broke the surface of the water. As it dove back under, its tail flipped up high in the air.

"Ooohhh!" the Aldens said at once.

"Keep your eyes peeled," Charlie said. "You're apt to see more."

"They're migrating south to warmer waters," Kate added.

Although they looked and looked, that was the only whale they saw.

Later, Charlie reeled in the nets. Fish flipped and flapped on the deck. The Aldens had never seen so many fish.

"These fish have to be sorted according to kind," Kate said.

"That's easy," Henry said.

But, with the fish slipping and sliding, it was more difficult than it looked. Still, they were able to do the job.

"Now put them here," Kate directed. She opened the tops of containers built into the deck. "These are the fish wells."

Charlie turned the boat around. "Time to move to another spot," he said.

By now, the fog had completely lifted. The water sparkled. The sky was clear blue. As they glided nearer to the Golden Gate Bridge, Jessie tilted her head to look up at it. It was so graceful, yet so sturdy. She thought about the people on the bridge. Soon she would be one of them.

Suddenly the engine sputtered and stopped. Kate raced to Charlie's side. "What's wrong?"

"The gauge reads empty," Charlie said. "We're out of fuel."

"You filled the tank last night," Henry said.

"Maybe the gauge is stuck," Jessie suggested.

Charlie tapped the gauge. The needle didn't move.

"Could be a leak." He went to check the tank. It was in good condition. No holes or loose fittings.

"Someone's siphoned off the fuel," Charlie concluded.

"Why would anyone want to do that?" Violet asked

"They wanted us to be stuck out here," Kate answered.

"But no one was near your boat last night until you came back," Henry said.

"Yes," Jessie added. "We saw your light."

Charlie looked surprised. "Light? I didn't use a light. I know this wharf like the back of my hand. I don't need a light. A little moonlight's all I need."

"Then someone *was* at the dock last night!" Henry concluded.

Benny wasn't listening. He was squinting toward shore. "How're we going to get back?" he said, his voice trembling a little.

Kate put an arm around his shoulders and pulled him close. "Don't worry, Benny. We'll call the Coast Guard on the radio. They'll come get us." She went inside the cabin.

Benny relaxed. "Good thing you have a radio, Charlie," he said.

"We couldn't go out without one," Charlie told him. "We never know when we'll need help."

Kate came back outside. They looked at her expectantly. "The radio's not working," she said. "One of the wires has been cut."

Violet's eyes grew wide. "We're stuck out here," she said.

"We're drifting farther away from the bridge!" Jessie said.

Then they heard a splash. Charlie had dropped the anchor.

"Now we won't go anywhere," he said. "We'll just sit here and wait. Someone will see us and come to help."

They sat for a long time. No one came to help.

Finally Henry saw a sailboat. It seemed to be coming their way. "Violet, quick! Give me your jacket," he said.

Violet handed him her pale lavender windbreaker.

"Your jacket is the lightest color," he explained. "Maybe they'll see it." He waved it above his head.

The boat moved farther away.

"It's going the other way," Jessie said. Disappointed, Henry lowered the jacket.

"I might have a flare," Charlie said, and he went inside the cabin to look. The others searched for something they could use to attract attention.

"Ahoy there!" someone called.

Benny ran to the rail. "It's Joe!"

Sure enough: Joe Martin's boat was

moving toward them. They all waved and shouted.

Joe cut his engine and drifted in. "What's the trouble?"

"We've run out of gas!" Benny shouted.

"And the radio's dead," Kate added.

"I'll go ashore and bring back some fuel," Joe offered.

"Can you take the children with you?" Charlie asked.

"Sure thing." Joe threw a line onto Charlie's boat. Kate caught it.

The boats were pulled side by side. "Benny, you go first," Henry directed.

"Watch your step," Joe said. He reached out his hand.

The boats pitched and rolled. When one bobbed up, the other dropped down.

This was not going to be easy. Benny took a deep breath. He grabbed hold of Joe's hand.

"Gotcha!" Joe said as Benny jumped into his arms.

Soon the other Aldens were aboard Joe's boat. Kate and Charlie stayed behind.

"I'll be back soon," Joe said as he nosed his boat away from *Charlie's Chum.*

"Lucky you were out here," Henry commented.

Joe smiled. "I was just coming in."

"Do you go out fishing more than once a day?" Henry asked.

Joe's smile faded. "No. Why?"

"Well, you went out twice yesterday," Henry said.

For a moment Joe looked confused. Then he smiled again. "Oh, yeah, right. When I brought in my catch, I noticed the engine seemed sluggish. I took her out later to check. That's when I saw Tony's boat."

"The engine seems fine now," Jessie said.

Joe nodded. "Probably my imagination."

Before long, the Aldens were back on shore. They waited on the pier for Charlie and Kate.

"Who do you suppose took the fuel?" Jessie asked.

Henry shrugged. "It was the person we saw last night. That's the only thing I'm sure of."

Violet and Benny said, "What person?"

Henry explained about the noise and the light he and Jessie had seen. "But it was too dark to tell who it was," he concluded.

"This morning we thought it was Charlie returning to his boat," Jessie said. "But then he told us that he didn't use a light."

"Maybe it was that mysterious man you keep seeing," Benny teased. He hadn't seen the man and wasn't sure he really existed.

Soon Charlie swung his boat up to the dock. Henry caught Charlie's line and tied it to a post. Kate and Charlie hopped onto the deck as Vito Marino trotted up.

"How was your catch?" he asked Charlie. "The restaurant is completely booked for tonight."

"We had a little trouble," Charlie said. "It shortened our day. I'll bring you our catch as soon as I prepare it."

"Show it to me now!" Vito insisted.

Charlie swung back aboard. Vito followed him. In no time, Vito was back on the dock, complaining.

"You can't say they aren't fresh," Charlie told him.

"They might be fresh, but there aren't enough of them to fill tonight's dinner orders," Vito snapped. "I'm telling you, Charlie, I can't deal with this." He stormed off.

Tony and Joe came up to find out what was happening. Kate explained.

"If anything else happens, I'll lose the account," Charlie said.

Joe's face clouded. "That's too bad, Charlie. That's a good account. Vito's is popular. He uses lots of fish."

Tony nodded. "I'd give anything if Vito would buy fish from me."

They all returned to prepare their boats for the next day. The Aldens waited nearby for Aunt Jane and Uncle Andy.

"Do you suppose Joe or Tony is causing the trouble?" Violet asked.

"They each have a motive," Henry said. "If Vito doesn't buy from Charlie, he might buy from one of them."

"It can't be Joe," Violet said. "He's too nice."

"Right," Benny agreed. "He took Tony out to get his boat, and he rescued us. Guilty people aren't *that* nice."

"Tony can't be the one," Jessie said. "Someone let his boat go. He wouldn't do that himself."

"He might have done it so no one would suspect him," Violet suggested.

"Or maybe Joe was right: Tony's knot came undone and the boat just drifted away," Benny said.

"Tony *was* on the wharf last night," Henry said. "He slept on his boat, remember? He could've sneaked onto the *Chum* before Charlie came back here."

"And he did say he'd give anything if Vito would buy fish from him," Jessie said.

Benny nodded. "He probably took the gas and broke the radio."

"There's that strange man," Henry said.

"Maybe he has nothing to do with the trouble, Henry," Violet said. "Just because he hangs around the wharf doesn't mean — "

"No, no," Henry interrupted. "I mean: *There he is!*"

They followed his gaze. The man stood against a wooden shack at the other end of the wharf. His sunglasses glinted in the light.

This time everyone — even Benny — saw him.

CHAPTER 7

Another Sighting

"What are you looking at?" a voice asked.

It was Aunt Jane.

"We keep seeing that man," Henry explained. "We've been thinking he might have something to do with the trouble."

Aunt Jane looked around. "What man?"

Jessie said, "He's over there."

But he wasn't. He had disappeared again.

"You children shouldn't worry about these things," Aunt Jane said. "Let Charlie and the other fishermen take care of it."

"But we're very good detectives," Benny said. "We've had lots of experience."

"Even detectives need time off, Benny," Aunt Jane said. She held up a bag. "I've brought lunch," she told them.

After the morning's fishing, they were all hungry.

"Where's Uncle Andy?" Jessie asked.

"Working," she answered. "After lunch, we'll take the ferry to Sausalito. Uncle Andy will meet us there later, and we'll drive home across the Golden Gate Bridge."

Jessie was especially happy to hear that. "Sounds great!" she said.

"There's Kate!" Henry said.

Waving, Kate headed their way.

"Let's ask her if she wants to go to Sausalito with us," Aunt Jane suggested. The Aldens liked that idea.

Kate couldn't go. "I have studying to do," she said. "But I have an invitation for you. Charlie wants you to come fishing tomorrow. He feels you were cheated today because of the trouble."

"May we go, Aunt Jane?" Jessie asked.

"I don't see why not," Aunt Jane said.

"And you can stay with me again," Kate said.

"Oh, but if you have studying to do . . ." Aunt Jane objected.

"I have all afternoon to study," Kate assured her.

"Well, okay, then. It's nice of you to ask, Kate," Aunt Jane said.

Benny hopped on one foot. "Oh, good! We can stay!"

"I'll meet you back here later," Kate said, and hurried away.

Aunt Jane and the children found a bench near the water. They ate peanut butter sandwiches, homemade chocolate chip cookies, and milk. Terns and gulls hovered overhead. When Benny dropped a bit of bread, one swooped in and caught it before it touched the ground.

Violet squinted, looking across the water. "Where is Sausalito?"

Aunt Jane pointed out a hill across the bay. "It's only a twenty-minute ferry ride," she said.

Henry collected the trash and dropped it into a can. "Are we ready?" he asked.

They walked along the waterfront to the ferry landing. "Looks like we just missed a ferry," Jessie said.

"They run often," Aunt Jane told her.

Waiting there, where the scenery was so beautiful, did not seem like waiting at all. Before long, a line formed behind them. Soon another boat was ready to make the trip.

Benny was the first down the long ramp. "Can we go to the top?" he asked.

"You children run along," Aunt Jane said. "I'm going to stay inside out of the wind."

The children clambered up the narrow stairway. "Be careful," Aunt Jane called after them.

They took positions along the upper rail. As they cruised across the bay, Violet pointed out a small island. Atop it was a big building. "What's that?" she asked.

"Alcatraz," Henry told her.

"What a funny name," Benny said.

Henry had read about the island. He

knew its history. "In the beginning, no one lived there but pelicans."

"Look!" Violet said. "There're some now!" Sure enough, squat, brown pelicans floated nearby.

"That's how it got its name," Henry continued. "*Alcatraces* means 'pelicans' in Spanish. A long time ago, soldiers were stationed there. Later, it became a prison."

Benny pulled his jacket tight around him. "A cold and windy prison," he said.

Jessie pointed to a hill ahead. There were colorful houses on its steep slope. "That must be Sausalito," she said.

The ferry nosed into the dock. Aunt Jane was waiting on the lower deck. They all followed the crowd onto the ramp. People were lined up, waiting for the return trip.

"There's Uncle Andy!" Aunt Jane said. "He must have finished his work early." She went on ahead to meet her husband.

Violet noticed a man and woman huddled together talking. She poked Henry. "There's that strange man again," she whispered.

"And there's Kate!" Benny blurted. He was so surprised to see Kate in a yellow slicker, he didn't think to keep his voice quiet.

Jessie studied the two people. The girl had her hood up and was turned away. Jessie couldn't tell whether or not it was Kate. But she was sure the man was the one they kept seeing on Fisherman's Wharf.

"I'm going to try to get a look at that woman," Henry said. He threaded his way through the crowd. But it was too late. The woman and the man had already boarded the ferry.

"That was Kate, all right," Benny said.

"We can't be certain, Benny," Jessica said.

"She said she was going to study," Violet reminded her little brother.

"Suppose it *was* Kate," Henry said. "Why would she be meeting that man?"

"Maybe she and the man are causing all the trouble," Benny suggested. "They met to plan more bad stuff."

"But why would she meet him *here*?"

Jessie wondered aloud. "She knew we were coming."

Uncle Andy waved and called to them. "Hurry up, slowpokes!"

The Aldens quickened their pace. "Let's give this some thought," Henry said. "We'll talk about it later."

Uncle Andy and Aunt Jane led them to the main street. "This street is called Bridgeway," Uncle Andy said.

Lots of interesting shops were clustered along one side. Across the way, two elephant statues marked the entrance to a park. Beyond, yachts rocked in the blue waters of the marina.

"What does Sausalito mean?" Violet asked.

"*Sauces* in Spanish means 'willow trees,' " Uncle Andy explained.

"And *lito* means 'little,' " Henry said.

Benny looked around. "I don't see any willow trees," he said.

Uncle Andy laughed. "They must be here somewhere."

After a while, Benny said, "All this walking makes me — "

"Hungry," everyone else finished.

"Then it's time to go back," Aunt Jane said.

Uncle Andy led them to his car. "I thought you might like to eat dinner at Vito's."

"Vito's Vittles," Benny said, chuckling to himself.

Uncle Andy drove out of Sausalito to the main road. They rode through a tunnel and then they were on the Golden Gate Bridge.

Jessie didn't know where to look. To the west, the sun spread a golden path on the water. To the east, San Francisco was outlined against the brilliant sky. Straight ahead, the orange towers of the bridge rose high above them.

"Well, Jessie," Uncle Andy asked, "is it what you expected?"

"Much more," Jessie answered.

Back at the wharf, they parked and headed toward the restaurant.

On their way, they passed the docks. Kate and Charlie were on *Charlie's Chum*. Kate was not wearing a yellow slicker.

"How about dinner?" Uncle Andy called to them.

Charlie said, "Not tonight, thanks."

"I'd better help Charlie," Kate said.

But Charlie wouldn't hear of it. "You go along. I'm about finished here."

Kate joined them. "I am hungry," she said.

"Did you finish your studying?" Jessie asked.

"Every bit of it," Kate answered. "Seems I know more than I thought I did." She smiled broadly and looked them in the eye. Either she wasn't the person they had seen in Sausalito or she was a very good liar.

The restaurant was bustling with activity. Vito greeted them at the door. "I have the perfect table for you," he said, and he led them to a round table that looked out on the harbor. He handed menus all around.

"I suppose we shouldn't order fish," Henry said.

"Why not, Henry?" Aunt Jane asked.

Before Henry could answer, Vito said, "Not order fish? Vito's is known for its fish. What do you want? The catch of the day? Salmon? Tuna? Sea bass? You name it; I have it." Then he quickly walked away.

"That's strange," Jessie said.

"What is this about?" Uncle Andy asked.

"We ran out of fuel this morning," Kate explained, "and we had to cut the fishing short."

"And Vito told Charlie he wouldn't have enough fish for tonight's dinner," Henry concluded.

"Vito was really angry," Benny added.

Uncle Andy shrugged. "He seems to have all the fish he needs."

"Maybe he bought some from someone else," Violet suggested. Everyone sat and thought about the mystery.

Finally they opened their menus. They had a difficult time making a selection. Everything sounded so good. Each of them decided to order something different. That way they could sample many dishes.

Benny looked around the restaurant. Old anchors, wheels, and other boat gear hung on the walls. The window in the kitchen door was a round porthole.

Suddenly Benny pulled at Henry's sleeve. "There's that man again!" he muttered. Henry looked up in time to see the mysterious man at the round window. Jessie and Violet saw him, too.

The Aldens exchanged puzzled glances. Each wondered the same thing: *What is that man doing in the kitchen of Vito's Vittles?*

CHAPTER 8

Sounds in the Night

After dinner, Henry, Jessie, Violet, and Benny went back to Kate's boat. While they were relaxing on the boat deck, it began to rain.

"We should go inside," Kate said.

"But it isn't raining hard," Jessie said. "May we stay up here for a little bit longer?"

"Okay. I'll get your jackets," Kate said. When she came back with them, the children put on their jackets and Kate slipped into her black poncho.

"Do you have a yellow slicker?" Violet asked.

Kate looked at her. "A yellow slicker? No. Why?"

Violet's face reddened. "Oh . . . uh . . ."

"Yellow is Violet's favorite color," Benny piped up. "Next to purple."

It began to pour. "I guess it's time to turn in," Kate said.

Once the Aldens were settled for the night, they discussed the events of the day.

"Do you suppose Vito is in on this?" Jessie asked.

"Why would Vito be causing trouble for the fishermen?" Henry said. "He needs their fish."

"I don't know," Jessie said. "It just seemed odd seeing that mysterious man in Vito's kitchen."

"That's right," Violet said. "What was he doing there?"

"Maybe he's the one who sold fish to Vito," Benny suggested.

"I don't think he's a fisherman," Violet said. "Where would he get the fish?"

They all thought about that. Finally Jessie said, "Maybe he works for one of the fishermen."

"That's possible," Henry agreed. "He could be helping to ruin Charlie's business so Vito will buy from someone else."

"What about Kate?" Benny asked. "What was she doing in Sausalito with that man?"

"That wasn't Kate," Violet argued. "You heard her say she doesn't own a yellow slicker."

"Well, it *was* Kate we saw in Chinatown," Benny said.

"We can't be sure, Benny," Jessie said.

"What about the red hair?" Benny persisted.

After a silence, Violet said, "Benny, there are lots of people with hair like that. And San Francisco is a big city."

Jessie yawned. "This is getting way too complicated," she said.

* * *

Late that night, Benny awoke with a start. "What was that?" he whispered. There it was again: the noise that had awakened him.

At the window, Henry said, "I think someone's on Charlie's dock."

Beside him, Jessie murmured, "Someone is out there. See that light?"

Violet and Benny crept out of bed. Before they could reach the window, another sound cut through the silence.

Breaking glass!

"What's happening?" Benny asked.

"The light went out," Henry told him.

Jessie peered through the window. "I don't see anyone."

"It's too dark out there," Henry said as he returned to bed. "And we don't know our way around the dock very well. Let's check it out in the morning."

Benny climbed under the covers. "Maybe Charlie came back to sleep on the boat again."

"Charlie doesn't use a light," Henry reminded him.

"Maybe he needed one tonight," Violet said. "There's no moon."

"We'll have to wait until morning to find out," Jessie said.

The next morning, they awoke to the sound of foghorns.

Henry looked at the clock. "It's late," he said. "We'd better get moving."

They dressed quickly.

"I wonder if Kate's still sleeping," Violet said.

In the main cabin, Jessie had the answer. "She isn't here."

They went outside on the deck to look for her. She wasn't there, either. In the distance, a patch of yellow shone through the drifting fog.

Violet squinted through the haze. "Look!" she said. "It's the woman in the yellow slicker."

"And she's on Joe Martin's boat!" Jessie added.

Benny nodded. "It's Kate," he said. "She's in on this with Joe Martin."

"Let's go," Henry urged. "We'll see what she's up to."

They hurried inside, grabbed their jackets, dashed back outside, and hopped onto the dock. Then they raced along the walkway to Charlie's and Joe's pier.

The red-haired woman was gone!

"We should tell Charlie about Kate," Benny said.

"Tell him what?" Henry asked.

"That she and Joe Martin and that strange man are causing all the trouble," Benny answered.

"But we don't know for sure, Benny," Jessie said.

"Charlie would never believe us," Henry added.

"*I* don't even believe it," Violet said.

"Yoo-hoo!" someone called.

It was Kate. She hurried toward them.

"She's not wearing the yellow slicker," Violet observed.

"Maybe we *didn't* see her on Joe's boat," Violet said. "Maybe we didn't see anyone. Maybe it was a trick of the fog."

Kate came up beside them. She was carrying a shopping bag. "I bought sourdough bread — a San Francisco specialty — for our breakfast," she said. "And lots of good snacks for later."

From his boat, Charlie called, "Are you landlubbers ready to set sail?"

"What's a landlubber?" Benny whispered.

Henry answered, "Someone who lives on the land and doesn't know much about the sea."

Benny chuckled. "That's us."

Kate led the parade to the boat. Waiting his turn to board, Henry saw something glistening on the dock. He leaned over and picked it up. It was a piece of broken glass.

"Come on, Henry," Charlie urged him. "The fish are waiting."

Henry set the glass fragment on top of a barrel where no one would step on it. Then he hopped aboard.

"Is the radio fixed?" Violet asked. She didn't want to be stuck out in the water again.

"Fixed," Charlie said. "Everything's ship-shape." Charlie backed the *Chum* away from the dock. "This is going to be a good day. I can feel it in my bones."

The Aldens hoped he was right.

CHAPTER 9

The Fish That Got Away

It was a perfect day — even more beautiful than the day before had been. The sea was calm. The sky was bright. The fishing was good.

It was difficult to think about trouble on a day like this.

"You were right," Benny said to Charlie. "This *is* a very good day."

Even the birds knew it. They hovered over the boat, squawking. Benny and Violet tore bits of bread from the large loaf Kate had brought and tossed them to the gulls. The birds dipped and dived, snatching up the tidbits.

They were having such a good time that when Charlie said "Let's haul in the nets," they were disappointed.

"Are we going in already?" Benny asked.

Kate smiled. "No, Benny," she said. "But the nets are full. We'll empty them into the well and cast them out again."

Kate and the Aldens helped reel in the nets. Charlie whistled as they worked. Fish jumped and splashed. Many of them escaped to slip back into the cold waters.

"They're getting away!" Violet said.

"Don't worry," Charlie told her. "We have plenty to spare."

And then the nets were up out of the water.

Empty!

Charlie's mouth dropped open. Kate gasped. The Aldens stared in disbelief. But it was true. Except for the few fish that had gotten tangled, the nets were empty. Char-

lie ran his hands along the netting. He punched his fist through one large rip after another.

"This can't be," Kate said. "I checked those nets myself."

Charlie was too angry to speak. He turned the boat around and headed for shore. Kate and the Aldens kept silent, too.

Ashore, the word spread quickly. Before long, Vito Marino stormed onto the dock. "Is it true?" he demanded. "Did you come in empty, Charlie?"

Charlie looked at him long and hard. Then he turned away without answering.

"It's true," Kate said.

"This is the last straw," Vito said. "I'm sorry, Charlie, but I can't depend on you."

Joe Martin's boat eased up to the dock. "What's going on?" he asked as he threw a line over a post. Kate told him.

Joe hopped onto the deck beside Charlie. "Oh, Charlie, what bad luck." He turned to Vito. "I had a very good day. Maybe I could help out until Charlie gets back on his feet."

He ushered Vito onto his boat for a look at the catch.

Vito shook Joe's hand. "It's a deal, Joe," he said. "I'll buy your fish."

Charlie watched them silently with narrowed eyes.

"Don't let this get you down, Charlie," Kate said. "Come on. Let's repair the nets."

Charlie waved her away. "It's no use," he said. "I'm finished." With hunched shoulders and slow steps, he headed off the pier.

"Let's go after him," Benny murmured. "We can tell him what we know."

Henry held him back. "We have to think about this first."

Kate came up beside them. "I'm going after Charlie," she told him. "Will you be all right?"

Jessie nodded. "We'll be fine. You go ahead." Kate trotted away.

"Joe and Kate," Benny said. "They're the ones."

Violet looked sad. "I can't believe Kate has anything to do with this."

"She could have cut the nets this morning," Henry said.

"Or last night," Jessie said. "She might have been the person we heard."

Henry nodded. "She had plenty of chances. She could have siphoned the gas and cut the radio wire, too."

Jessie agreed. "No one would suspect anything if they saw her on Charlie's boat."

"If she *is* working with Joe, it would all make sense," Henry said. "Joe wanted Vito's business; she helped him get it."

"But what about Tony?" Violet asked. "He said he'd give anything to get Vito's business. And don't forget Vito and that strange man. Maybe they were planning all this last night in the restaurant kitchen."

Benny nodded. "All of them — they're all in on it."

"We have to tell Charlie," Jessie said.

Henry shook his head. "He'll never believe us — not without proof."

"Well, then, let's get some," Benny suggested.

"We'll start right here," Henry said. He

began walking along Charlie's and Joe's dock. "Look for anything strange," he directed the others. "Anything that looks out of place."

Jessie and Violet stepped onto *Charlie's Chum*. They poked in boxes and peered under seats. On the pier, Henry moved alongside the boat, his eyes downcast. He found nothing but the glass fragment he had seen that morning.

Across from him, Benny examined Joe's side of the dock. "There's nothing here," Benny said at last. Then he noticed something inside a coil of rope. "Oh, wait." He pulled the rope aside. "Forget it," he said. "It's just an old lantern like the one we use when we go camping."

"Let's walk along the wharf," Jessie suggested. "We might find some clue there." But they found nothing.

Finally Henry said, "Proof or no proof, I think we have to tell Charlie what we think."

"But you said he won't believe us," Violet reminded him.

"We'll have to convince him," Henry said.

"Maybe he can put the puzzle together," Jessie added.

Thinking Charlie might have returned to the boat, they doubled back. He wasn't there.

"Let's go get some lunch. We can talk more about what we know," Henry said. They decided to go to Pier 39.

When they were nearly there, they stopped short. Ahead of them, at the pier entrance, two men stood talking.

One of the men was Charlie. The other was the mysterious man! The Aldens ducked around a corner so Charlie wouldn't see them.

"What could Charlie be talking to that man about?" Benny wondered aloud.

"Maybe he found out the man has something to do with all the trouble," Violet suggested, "and he's telling him to stop."

"That's possible," Henry said.

"It's also possible that Charlie is *part* of the problem," Jessie said.

"Charlie?" Violet sounded surprised. "But most of the bad things have been happening to *him*."

No one could deny that.

"Well, one thing is sure," Henry said. "We can't tell Charlie what we suspect. Not now. Not until we know more."

"We'll keep looking for proof after we eat," Jessie said.

They ordered pizza in one of the many pier restaurants. Waiting for their order, each Alden was silent, thinking.

"I wonder where Tony was," Jessie said at last.

"When?" Henry asked.

"Just now when we came back to shore."

"He's probably still out fishing," Violet suggested.

"But every other time there was trouble, he was there," Jessie reminded them. "Joe, Vito, Tony — they were all there."

Benny's eyes widened. "Maybe he cut the nets, and he didn't want to be around when Charlie found out."

"But if he did it to get Vito's business,

he'd want to be there when Vito came along," Jessie said.

"That's right," Violet said. "Joe was there, so he got the business."

The pizza arrived. For a while, they were too busy eating to talk. When they had nearly finished, Henry said, "We should stop thinking and talking about the trouble on the wharf."

"Why?" Benny wanted to know.

"You can think about something too hard," Henry explained. "Sometimes, if you put a problem in the back of your mind, the answer just . . . pops up."

"Oh, I get it," Benny said. "It's there all the time, but you can't see it."

They all thought Henry might be right.

"But if we don't talk about the mystery," Benny said, "what should we talk about?"

"About the things we still want to see," Henry answered. He pulled the rolled guidebook from his back pocket. "There are so many interesting places in San Francisco. We've only been to a few."

"Golden Gate Park is something we should see," Jessie said.

Henry agreed. "That's one I've marked. Especially the Academy of Sciences. There's a planetarium there and an aquarium."

"More *fish*?" Benny said. "Haven't we seen enough of those?"

"They have a Touch Tide Pool, Benny, where you can actually hold starfish and sea urchins." He opened the book and read aloud from it.

"The Japanese Tea Gardens sound interesting," Violet said.

"We could spend the whole day in the park," Jessie said. "There's so much to see. We'll make a list and give it to Uncle Andy," she decided.

CHAPTER 10

The Catch of the Day

When they returned to the docks, the Aldens met Kate.

"I've been looking for you," she said. "Your aunt phoned. She and your uncle will be late. They don't expect to get here until dinnertime. I wish I had time to take you sightseeing, but with Charlie and all . . ." Her voice trailed off.

"We'll find plenty to do," Jessie assured her.

"How *is* Charlie?" Henry asked.

Kate shrugged. "He wanted to be alone,"

she said. Her green eyes were sad.

"Alone?" Benny repeated. "But we just saw him with — "

Jessie gave him a poke.

"It's not at all like him," Kate continued. "I'm going to find him now and try to talk to him. See you later," she said, and started away.

Kate could not be involved in the trouble. She was too nice, too concerned about other people. The person they had seen in Chinatown, Sausalito, and on Joe Martin's boat wasn't Kate. Violet was sure of it.

"She didn't do it," Violet murmured.

Benny didn't like to see Violet upset. To make her feel better, he said, "If Kate did do it, she probably had a really good reason."

But it didn't work. "You all think she's guilty," Violet said. "And now you think Charlie's in on it, too."

"We don't know for sure," Jessie said. "We're just trying to figure it out."

Henry put an arm around Violet's shoulders. "We hope Kate and Charlie have nothing to do with all this," he said. "We hope nobody we know is involved."

"Yes," Jessie added. "Joe and Tony — they're good people, too. It's hard to believe either of them could be guilty."

Even Violet had to agree that was true.

"If we knew more about the mysterious man," Henry said, "we might be able to solve this puzzle."

They decided to look for the man.

"What will we do if we find him?" Benny asked.

"We'll decide that when the time comes," Jessie answered.

The time never came. They looked all over the piers, but they could not find the mysterious man.

Just before sunset, they gathered on the wharf. Charlie was himself again, friendly and positive. He and Kate were repairing the torn nets.

The Aldens wondered if his good mood

might have had something to do with his meeting with the mysterious man earlier in the day.

Tony Gregor was helping Kate and Charlie. *If he had cut the nets, why would he help repair them?* Henry wondered.

"Has anyone seen Joe?" Tony asked.

Charlie shrugged. "Not since he brought in his catch."

"Perfect timing, too," Kate added, "with Vito ready to buy."

"Here comes Joe," Benny said.

Joe Martin sauntered toward them, a big smile on his face.

Looking at him, the Aldens thought it was hard to believe that he had anything to do with the trouble on the wharf. He had helped Tony rescue his boat; he had brought the Aldens to shore when they were stranded; and he had returned to the *Chum* with fuel. And, even today, when he sold Vito his catch, he had said, "Maybe I could help out until Charlie gets back on his feet." That didn't sound like a man who was trying to steal Charlie's business.

"Hey, there," Joe said. "This looks like a party."

"It's a repair-the-torn-net party," Charlie said. "Want to help?"

Joe's smile faded. "Wish I could," he said, "but I have some work of my own." He went down the dock to his boat and disappeared inside. A few minutes later, he was back. "Charlie, do you have a lantern I could borrow? It's getting too dark to work without one, and I can't find mine."

Benny remembered the lantern in the coil of rope. He said, "But we saw — "

Henry remembered the lantern, too. "I'll get you a light," he interrupted, and dashed away.

"Do you know where my lantern is?" Charlie called after Henry.

"Don't worry, Charlie," Benny said. "He'll find a light."

Henry was back in a flash, carrying a lantern.

"That's not my lantern," Charlie said.

"I think Joe knows who owns it," Henry said. He held up a piece of broken glass.

"And I think he knows who owns this, too." He turned the lantern to reveal a hole the shape of the broken glass.

Joe's smile froze. "I . . . uh . . . "

"We heard glass breaking out on the dock last night," Violet said.

Charlie glared at Joe. "So you were the one who ripped these nets."

Joe backed away. "No, no. Not me. I didn't do it."

"And you siphoned off our fuel and broke the radio," Kate said.

"No, listen," Joe pleaded. "I didn't do any of those things. I *did* break my lantern. I came back here last night to check on my boat. I tripped over something and the lantern fell."

Jessie said, "But you said you couldn't find your lantern."

Joe seemed to be searching for a reply. Finally he said, "I . . . uh . . . I was embarrassed. What kind of fisherman breaks his lantern?"

"A greedy fisherman." The words came from behind them.

The Aldens whirled around.

The voice belonged to Kate!

That couldn't be. Kate was beside them. Yet the faces were the same; the red hair was the same. But this woman wore a yellow slicker.

"Two Kates!" Benny exclaimed.

Kate was no less surprised. "Kim!" she cried. "What are you doing here?"

The other woman said, "Before I tell you that, let me introduce Sam Goodall." She gestured toward the man beside her.

The mysterious man!

"He's an investigator," Kim continued.

Sam Goodall stepped forward. "Some of the fishermen hired me to find out who was causing the trouble on the wharf," he explained. "I suspected you, Joe, from the beginning, but I could never find the proof." He turned to the Aldens. "The lantern is just what I needed to close this case, and I have you kids to thank for that."

Joe Martin raised his arms into the air. "All right," he said. "I did it. I didn't mean to ruin anyone's business. I just wanted to show that I could be as good as the other fishermen. But how could I compete with men like Charlie and Tony?"

"It takes years of practice," Kate told him. "You've only just started."

Sam Goodall glanced at Charlie and Tony. "What do you want to do about this?"

"Joe should pay for what he's done," Tony said.

Charlie thought about that. "Joe has the makings of a good fisherman," he said. "But he has to learn to have patience. If he works for us for a while, we can teach him. And he'll be making up for our losses at the same time. What do you think, Tony?"

"Great idea, Charlie," Tony answered. "I think the other fishermen will agree."

Then Sam took Joe aside to ask him a few more questions.

Now only one mystery remained: Who was the young woman in the yellow slicker?

Kate answered that question. "This is my

twin sister, Kim," she said. "She's studying to be a private investigator."

"I'm very happy to meet you, Kim," Violet said, and then she looked at her brothers and sister. Her expression said, *I told you so.*

"She'll have to tell you what she's doing here," Kate continued, "because I haven't the slightest idea."

"Sam asked me to help out," Kim explained. "I took a job delivering fish for Joe. That way I could keep an eye on him."

"But why didn't you tell me?" Kate asked.

"I asked her not to," Sam answered. "The fewer people who knew, the better."

"Believe me, Kate," Kim said, "it wasn't easy. I *wanted* to tell you. Talk about patience!"

"But Joe must've known you were Kate's twin," Charlie said. "And he never mentioned it."

"I asked him not to," Kim explained. "I told him Kate and I were having some problems and she'd be upset if she knew I was working down here."

"Were you delivering fish in Chinatown?" Henry asked.

Kim nodded. "Joe has been supplying one of the restaurants there."

"What about Sausalito?" Violet asked.

Kim looked surprised. "You saw me in Sausalito?"

"Yes," Benny answered. "But we thought you were Kate."

"*I* didn't think so," Violet said.

Kim nodded. "I was delivering fish there, too."

"We saw *you* there, too," Benny told Sam.

"I decided to go along," Sam said. "It gave us the chance to exchange information. We couldn't risk being seen together. We figured no one would see us there."

"But you were wrong," Benny piped up.

Sam laughed. "We didn't know you were such good detectives."

"We've had lots of practice," Benny said.

Vito Marino came running toward them. "I just heard about Joe. Is it true?"

Charlie explained what had happened. Vito was upset. "What are we going to do about this?" he asked.

"We're going to teach Joe the importance of honesty," Tony said.

Shortly thereafter, Aunt Jane and Uncle Andy arrived.

"Is everyone ready for dinner?" Aunt Jane asked.

"We sure are," Benny answered.

Vito said, "Come to my place. Dinner's on me." He turned to Joe. "You're not charging me for those fish you brought in this morning, are you, Joe?"

Joe shook his head. "No. They're my gift to you," he mumbled. "It's the least I can do."

Kate introduced the Beans to her sister, Kim, and to Sam Goodall. Then everyone — except Joe, who stayed behind to repair the nets — headed for Vito's Vittles. On the way there, the Aldens excitedly discussed the events of the day.

In the distance, the sky was a brilliant red. The lights on the Golden Gate Bridge looked like bright beads strung across the bay. This was truly a beautiful city. And there was so much of it left to see.

"So, Vito, what's the catch of the day?" Uncle Andy asked.

The Aldens smiled at one another. They had just helped uncover a troublemaker. That was the real catch of the day.

Laughing, Jessie said, "It was a big one, Uncle Andy. A really big one!"

GERTRUDE CHANDLER WARNER discovered when she was teaching that many readers who like an exciting story could find no books that were both easy and fun to read. She decided to try to meet this need, and her first book, *The Boxcar Children*, quickly proved she had succeeded.

Miss Warner drew on her own experiences to write the mystery. As a child she spent hours watching trains go by on the tracks opposite her family home. She often dreamed about what it would be like to set up housekeeping in a caboose or freight car — the situation the Alden children find themselves in.

When Miss Warner received requests for more adventures involving Henry, Jessie, Violet, and Benny Alden, she began additional stories. In each, she chose a special setting and introduced unusual or eccentric characters who liked the unpredictable.

While the mystery element is central to each of Miss Warner's books, she never thought of them as strictly juvenile mysteries. She liked to stress the Aldens' independence and resourcefulness and their solid New England devotion to using up and making do. The Aldens go about most of their adventures with as little adult supervision as possible — something else that delights young readers.

Miss Warner lived in Putnam, Connecticut, until her death in 1979. During her lifetime, she received hundreds of letters from girls and boys telling her how much they liked her books.